About the Author

Mary Hayley Bell was born in Shanghai and spent most of her early youth in China. She was on the stage for some years, but when she married actor and producer John Mills she gave up her career and devoted her time to raising a family of two daughters, Juliet and Hayley, and a son, Jonathan. Besides five stage plays produced in the West End of London, she has written her autobiography and three novels. *Whistle Down the Wind* was made into a successful film in 1961 with her daughter Hayley in the leading role, and is now the subject of a musical by Andrew Lloyd Webber.

Whistle Down the Wind

Mary Hayley Bell

Illustrations by Ōven Edwards

*Hodder
Children's
Books*

a division of Hodder Headline plc

For Bunch, Bags and Noony

Copyright © 1958 by Hayley Bell Productions, Limited
Illustrations copyright © 1997

First published in 1958 by T.V. Boardman & Company Limited
Published in 1989 by Chivers Press
This edition published in 1997 by Hodder Children's Books
A Division of Hodder Headline PLC

The right of Mary Hayley Bell to be identified as the Author of
the Work has been asserted by her in accordance with the
Copyright, Designs and Patents Act 1988.

10 9 8 7 6 5 4 3 2

A CIP catalogue record for this book is
available from the British Library

ISBN 0 340 71496 4

Typeset by Palimpsest Book Production Limited,
Polmont, Stirlingshire

Printed and bound in Great Britain by
Clays Ltd, St Ives plc

Hodder Children's Books
a division of Hodder Headline plc
338 Euston Road
London NW1 3BH

One

I am ten, and they call me Brat.

Of course that isn't my right name, nobody could be christened with a name like that.

All our lousy first names are birds' names. Don't ask me why. I imagine our mother was keen on birds and flying, though I don't know much about her. She flew off some years ago with this character called Peregrine. She lives in South Africa, on a different kind of farm, and once in a way we get a Christmas card – which is quite useful, as we keep the stamp.

Going back to our names. You may as well get them straight and then forget them – all except for Swallow. She's the eldest, and for some good reason still hangs onto this Swallow name; most likely because – let's face it – it's certainly the nicest.

On account of living on this farm, and having birds' names, of course we know all about animals and birds and the facts of life and all that. Well, you have to, don't you?

Swallow – she's twelve. I like her. Most people do, and she's the only kind of mother we've ever known – right down to washing socks and knickers and getting you out of your wellingtons when they're full of warm water, and you're enjoying standing about.

'Swallow, much favoured of the poets', the books say, and the description of her as a bird isn't too far wrong, not really: 'skimming low over ponds, or flying with speed and grace', that *could* be her. Also this 'high metallic voice', that's her, though I like it. It kills me.

Coming, next, to me. Get this. Of all lousy names – mine is Brambling!

Well, it's lucky I don't go to boarding school, that's all. Brambling! I mean, why not Bombay Duck?

Bet you never heard of it. Bet you've no idea that it's a sort of chaffinch. Just a brown bird. That's all. Its haunts are fields and woods, and it makes a 'wee or tak noise not often noticed'. You can say that again, because I can talk myself to a standstill sometimes and no one takes the blindest bit of notice.

On the whole I prefer to be called Brat.

Now we come to Poor Baby. Poor Baby, I'd like you to know, is my brother. As long as I can remember he's been called Poor Baby. Cookie started it, and you *could* say he needs a mother.

His real name is Merlin, which of course means 'the littlest falcon', but you knew that.

No one ever calls him that except Granny.

He's seven. He smokes and rolls his own cigarettes.

He's thin, like a blade of grass, with a great chunk of red hair on his head, and goes everywhere like the wind. He could have been called Shag just as easily; you know – this cormorant-type bird.

Well, he wasn't. 'Merlin' he was saddled with, though of course he never answers to it. In the book it's pretty true what it says about him: 'Swift on the wing and out-flying his victim.' Also, his note is a 'chattering scream'.

Golly, you can say that again.

There's only one person who can outstrip him, and that's Bette Davis.

She's a white Pekinese about seven inches long. She'll never get any bigger.

She got sucked into the Hoover last week.

There are other dogs about the joint like Hamlet and Charlie Staircase, but Bette Davis deserves the most mention, as she's the corniest.

That's us.

Then there's Father.

Quite honestly we don't see too much of Father. He's up early with this milking lark, and all day he has something on his mind that's all his own.

He's nice. We like him all right. He laughs a lot, and when we let him in on this Big Secret that I'm going to tell you about – well, he was wonderful. He was really.

There's Cookie.

She's Canadian, which is maybe why we talk in a queerish way.

She's all right too. She imagines she has some lousy disease, she doesn't know what.

Every now and again she hits the part of her back she can't reach with a clothes-brush or an Alka-Seltzer bottle. Nellie is one of us too. She hoovers.

Sometimes the Land-Rover is late picking us up from school – well, we could say *always* late. So tell you what we do. We go to Smith's, the bookshop. Poor Baby reads *Beano* and *Dandy*. Myself, I like horse books. I've been reading a chapter every day now for a week.

Hope to God the book isn't sold before I've finished it.

Funny thing, Swallow doesn't read anything in Smith's; she collects ladybirds. There are hundreds of them. They crawl all over Swallow. She reckons she's the queen of the ladybirds, and when she gets into the Land-Rover, with Edward in front, she literally looks like she's got measles.

Tell you what I like – Alka-Seltzer. I could live on it, and mostly do.

Right next to Smith's is Boots. I just go in and ask for an Alka-Seltzer. The man in there has huge sticking-out eyebrows; I saw him once with a cap on, and those damned eyebrows curled right out in front of his cap. Made him look madly corny. Well, when I ask him for an Alka-Seltzer these eyebrows shoot, but he never argues. I always get it.

Tell you what I don't like – dustbins.

I have a horror of death. Every night I think I'm going to die when the light goes out. Cookie says it's gas, and to lie on my stomach. Dustbins have something to do with death. I hate to see glowing bits of apple peel all yellow and mixed up with bacon rind and cinders.

It's an odd thing, but grown-ups don't seem to worry about those things at all. Now we're on the subject of grown-ups, generally speaking I think they're mad.

I prefer kids, I do really.

Grown-ups kill me. They make so much out of nothing; and all that drink that turns them into idiots, laughing like crazy about nothing at all.

I often wonder if they realise how awful they smell when they kiss you goodnight.

4

Swallow and Poor Baby and me, we reel, but reel, against the stairs after we've said goodnight.

As I said, I prefer kids. They're more balanced; I mean, they really are. You see these grown-ups, heavy and downhearted about taxis and the state of the world.

'Why do they take a taxi?' Poor Baby says – and he's right.

Then suddenly someone says 'Let's have a drink', and they get at that golden-looking bottle with the funny smell in it, and in a moment they're changed people: dancing on the table, standing on the back of the sofa with funny hats on, playing the piano with the loud pedal down; laughing like maniacs at nothing, but nothing!

On top of that, they suddenly notice us; get all serious and shout *'Bed'* in a ferocious voice.

That's when they kiss you and you get that awful smell.

I'm glad I'm a kid; I think they have more sense.

I mean, these grown-ups are always on about the state of the world, but *always*. Well, aren't they? But watch as you can, they never *do* anything about it to put it right.

These newspapers drive them nuts.

'I'm going to write to *The Times*!' they shout.

But you know they never do.

These bombs, and murders, and lunatics at large, and polio injections – constipation, and the doctors under the control of the drug-makers; all through lunch one day they blinded and cursed about them.

That's when they get at this golden bottle. Then they don't seem to be mad any more and just start laughing.

I give up. I do really.

I can't admire grown-ups. I think they're awful.

5

Except for people like Edward. He works with father and knows more about trees and flowers and insects than anyone living, I should think.

It was that weekend (you know, the Big Secret I was going to tell you about) at breakfast we were discussing them.

'What's wrong with these grown-ups?' I said to Poor Baby.

He didn't answer. He was feeding Bette Davis with her prunes and Wheat Germ. (She has it every day, and *she* has no problem with constipation, I can tell you.)

'What's wrong with these grown-ups?' I said to Swallow.

'No purpose,' Swallow said. She was eating prunes and Wheat Germ too.

'No wars to fight. Miss D. says we're at our best when we have wars to fight or there's wholesale unemployment.'

'Why?'

'Because it brings out the best in them, Miss D. says. Without wars to fight and wholesale unemployment there's no purpose.'

'What's purpose, anyway?' Poor Baby was up off the floor by now.

'Purpose? . . . Well, God or Jesus – if He came back right now, p'raps—'

'Poor Jesus! He couldn't *walk*!' Poor Baby made a ghastly face.

'What d'you mean, He couldn't walk?' I didn't get his trend.

'Well, for heaven's sake, Brat! When I stuck a pitchfork into my foot it was bad enough, but those *nails*! Ouch!'

Swallow had a bit of bacon rind on her fork. It looked like a worm that couldn't save itself.

'What about the Vicar? Why don't people ask the Vicar what to do?' Poor Baby was under the table again.

'I don't understand half what he talks about.' I said it and I meant it. 'Look at that sermon. I remember every word of it, and not one word made sense. Listen—'

I got up onto a chair to feel more like the Vicar.

'Oh, place me upon a rock that is higher than me.'

'I' – Swallow is rather proud of her English.

'Oh, place me upon a rock that is higher than I. . . . Now, my friends, what does that mean? Oh, place me . . . on a rock . . . that is higher, than I. . . . It means simply, my friends, that that rock is higher than I . . . that is to say, it is out of reach . . . and that I must reach it. . . .'

'Why doesn't he climb up?' Poor Baby had two pieces of bacon rind.

'And if someone placed him up there, he'd be going on about someone else getting him down! It doesn't make sense, it doesn't really. Let's face it, you get no help or understanding from any grown-ups at all, you don't really.'

'All the same, I quite like the Vicar.' Swallow had finished her bit of rind. 'Remember when we took all the dogs to church and filled up a whole pew? He never turned a hair.'

Actually he directed his whole sermon to this poodle, Charlie Staircase, who never took his eyes off the pulpit.

'As grown-ups go I think the Vicar goes pretty well,' said Poor Baby.

At any moment he was going to burn himself on this hotplate.

I got down from my chair.

'I think they're all pretty corny.' And that was my final word.

Elfred, the gardener's boy, was in the shed when I went outside. He's worn the same suit for five years, and when he bends down to do anything his trousers pinch him behind the knees, so he's always saying 'Aioutch'. That's where Poor Baby gets the expression from.

'That Elizabeth is looking for you,' he said.

Elizabeth is here most every day. She's the only girl Poor Baby really cares about.

She's frightfully religious. She's five.

Sometimes when she gets carried away with her subject her face goes practically puce and her eyes purple. When she gets on to religion, phew! You have to give it to her, she knows her subject. You just can't stump her. God actually speaks to her, and in fact the whole of this Big Secret was started by her. It's really the whole point of this story, because it was such a tremendous *thing*, such an Experience, that it can't go unrecorded.

She comes in this Land-Rover with us to school, this Elizabeth. Her people have a market garden, and in the summer her wretched mother stands for hours by this stall selling these tomatoes and things.

So I went off. Not that I particularly wanted Elizabeth. Well, she's five, like I told you; but I knew if I stayed in the shed I'd have to sit on the wood Elfred was chopping.

Elizabeth was feeding the goldfish with tomato seeds.

'Why you take so long over breakfast?' Her eyes were a bit purple again.

'We were having a discussion about grown-ups and Jesus,' I told her.

She threw a whole tomato in and stood up.

'I just missed Him.'

'Just missed who?' I was interested, vaguely.

'Jesus.' There were a few old dried bits of tomato on her hands. Disgusting really. I hate tomato.

'What you mean, you just missed Jesus?' I *was* interested now.

'Well—'

'Go on—'

'Remember that Palm Sunday procession?'

I nodded. Went on nodding, it helped my neck.

'Me and Samarel Damarel were sittin' on the wall watchin' the procession—' Something in her nose was itching, and she started picking at it. This made me restless.

'Well – go on.'

'I was sittin' up on this wall with her, waitin' – well, for hours – and I had to go and spend a penny. . . . Well, when I came back I said to Samarel Damarel, "Has He gone by yet?" and she said, all sort of excited: "*Yes!* You just missed Him." So that's how I missed Him.'

'What a swizz!'

'Yes, wasn't it?'

There wasn't any more to say really, so I went away. She wasn't waiting for me, anyway. She was waiting for Poor Baby.

She's frantically in love with him.

It was a misty morning – well, fog actually, but being in the country it was white. Everything was kind of queer – still – no kind of noise anywhere except Elfred hacking at this wood in the shed.

I was in a wandering mood. In this mood I'm liable to

be a crashing bore to everyone. Know why?—because I don't do anything definite for hours at a time. Just drool about, staring at people, and asking them questions that they don't want to answer. I knew I was in for one of these moods the moment I started asking questions at breakfast.

Mind you, I don't like it any more than anyone else. At best, I'll go off into the woods and make up some poetry.

At worst, I'll stand about and stare at people.

I was in the latter mood, and hiccoughs were coming on.

I sort of staggered down towards the cowsheds. It was a queer sort of day, all right. Very still, like I said before – kind of rainy, and damp, and the fog made it darkish, like it was evening already, and we hadn't even had lunch.

It was the beginning of the Big Secret – the one I said I'd tell you about. Only then I didn't know. I was just mouldy all over. I was really. I even thought of washing my hair for something to do.

Some purpose.

In the distance I could see the men hedging. The fire looked inviting and I thought, well, I'll go up there and ask *them* some questions. Maybe Poor Baby and Swallow will be there. I could even hear a tractor about ten miles off, it was so quiet.

I didn't go anywhere. I sat on the swing. It was wet. I could feel it through my jeans. I liked that. I wondered if I ought to go to my rooms and nail up my curtain that had fallen down. I didn't know where Poor Baby kept his hammer and nails.

He hides them from Cookie.

So I didn't do that either. I was just a mess. These hiccoughs had left me quite weak. I even wondered if I'd die in the daytime. Right now in fact – on the swing.

Then I saw Swallow. She was doing one of her skimming runs, the kind she does when she doesn't want anyone to see her.

I stopped the swing and watched her.

She disappeared into the barn.

I wondered. Just sat and wondered. I did really.

I was about to follow her when Poor Baby suddenly rushed past me towards the kitchen.

'What's going on? What's this?' I shouted.

'This is chaos,' he shouted back at me and disappeared.

Chaos?

I thought, I'll just wait till he comes back.

He was past me before I had time to think much. He had a whole lump of cake in his hand.

'Where you going with that?' I shouted again.

He never answered. He'd gone, like I told you. Like the wind.

I got off the swing. My drawers were sticking to me but I didn't care too much.

It was at this point that I saw Elizabeth.

She was walking slowly towards the house. She looked – well, ghastly really. Her face was scarlet and her eyes quite purple. Her legs were all scratched and bleeding, but I knew she didn't care, not with that look on her face.

Something had happened. Something ghastly, I should think. An accident, p'raps. Or a cow had had a baby that wasn't a cow and maybe a giraffe . . . something like that. I knew it was. It could only be some kind of disaster by the way Elizabeth looked.

I blocked her way. I got out my menacing look.

'Stop!' I said, very fierce.

She stopped.

'What is goin' on in the barn then, with Swallow skimming, and Poor Baby with a great hunk of cake in his hand? Tell at once, or I'll go and tell Cookie.'

She looked terrified, but terrified. I knew I had her in my cleft stick.

'Come on . . .' I said, sort of hoarse.

Her eyes were gigantic. I thought they were going to fall out.

She took a hell of a great deep breath, and held it. She was being one of those tortured prisoners of war who won't tell.

'I'll tell Cookie.' I started towards the kitchen.

'NO!' She hung onto my arm. I'm twice her size.

'Well?' I waited, one foot still in the air.

'It's Jesus,' she whispered, looking over her shoulder.

'What about Jesus?'

'He's come.' Her whisper was so small I could hardly hear.

'What d'you mean?'

'He's here, He's arrived.'

'Where is he, then?'

'In the barn.'

'Barn?'

'Yes, in the manger . . . with Bette Davis . . .'

Two

I didn't follow her into the barn. I stood around.

Jesus! In there!

P'raps I was afraid. I don't know. I don't think I was really. I mean, I didn't have any goose pimples about. My heart wasn't bothering me. Funny thing though, my hiccoughs had gone.

I stood on the swing and swung it about, crookedly, as fast as I could.

I was thinking of the others really. It was their Thing; they'd found Him, and fixed Him up with cake and Bette Davis. Like it was their game, and I'd asked if I could join in.

I wasn't going to dash in there all eager beaver.

I was going to think this Thing out; so I got a good idea in my head about old Jesus and what I expected to find in that manger.

Manger! Must be a baby, then!

So all right, if He was a baby, where was that old star and these wise men? And why weren't the farm boys here? – you know, shepherds, because we do have sheep around the joint too.

Of course, even if there *was* a star, you couldn't see it, not in this fog.

If you don't work hard on these swings they pretty soon stop swinging. This one had stopped.

I s'pose everyone has their own picture in their heads about what He looks like. I wondered what Dad's picture was.

And Granny? I'll bet Granny's picture is corny.

Edward's and Cookie's and Nellie's, and all those week-end guests. P'raps they don't have a picture at all.

The Vicar? What about the Vicar? I s'posed the Vicar's picture was all those stained-glass window jobs – long hair and beards, and trailing different-coloured sheets.

Unless, of course, this Jesus is a baby.

So how do they know it's Jesus because it's a baby?

Someone could have left it about. They're always doing it in the newspapers.

P'raps we can get a reward! Thousands, p'raps.

I got to thinking of my own picture of Him. Not a baby, of course. A man.

In my picture He always has a policeman's helmet on. Don't ask me why. And gigantic. Like Father Christmas.

Of course I know there isn't any Father Christmas. But I used to believe when I was young.

Swallow says if you *believe* in him – old Father Christmas, I mean – then he exists in *some* sort of way. If you don't, then he's just old Dad tripping over the carpet and cursing and blinding.

P'raps it's the same with Jesus. I never get the feeling that grown-ups believe in Him. P'raps they did when they were young – like Father Christmas.

Yet, I just remembered; only this morning Swallow said: if He comes again there might be a purpose.

Purpose for what?

I must get this word purpose straight. I'll look it up in the dictionary.

I got off the swing and started off to the house.

Suddenly I saw Poor Baby. He was on the run again. He stopped.

'Aren't you going into the barn to see Jesus?'

'No, I'm going into the house to look up "Purpose" in the dictionary.'

We walked up together.

'Where you going?' I asked him.

'To get my plasters. He's hurt hisself.'

Poor Baby has his own set of plasters. If you go and hack yourself anywhere you have to ask *him* for a plaster. They're the only ones in the house. He knows all the right sizes for the different cuts. He always has waterproof ones.

'Big plaster, or little?'

'Just the biggest in the tin. Maybe the whole tin.'

He stopped and picked something up. It was one of those bits of wood, like a toothpick with a lump of wool on either end.

'What's this?'

'It's a thing to clean your ears out with. Old Cocky was doing it yesterday.'

He threw it away, I'm glad to say.

'Why don't you go into the barn?'

'Don't want to.'

'Why?'

'Don't know.'

'It's quite interesting, really it is.'

'Why?'

'Don't know.'

He moved off, like he was in a hurry.

'Has Bette Davis got her newspaper?'

(It's the only thing she'll spend a penny on.)

'No. I'll take Jesus some comics, and when He's finished reading them Bette Davis can have them.'

'What's He doing now?'

'Sleeping, I think. He looks terribly tired. Maybe He's come a long way.'

'Where's He come from?'

'That's a thought, isn't it?'

He stood on the step thinking furiously.

'From Heaven, I s'pose.'

'Like a sort of Sputnik . . .'

'Yes . . . like that really. We'll ask Him when He wakes up.'

'Are Swallow and Elizabeth in there?'

'No. Swallow is washing His socks in the dairy, and Elizabeth has gone home to lunch.'

Then he went.

I thought maybe I *would* go into the barn. I could look in the dictionary later. The dictionary is always there.

It took me some time to find the right place. Well, I mean the barn is a hell of a big place. It's full of sacks of corn and things, different mushy food for calves, and old baskets. The place was full of these doves we keep. They're madly tame, and in the summer when we eat out they just damn well come and sit on the table; that's all very well, nobody minds them cracking away at the food, but they forget where they are and excuse themselves all over the table, even on the lettuce once. Granny was livid.

Well, there wasn't any sign of Jesus in the lower barn,

and I knew all the places to look, and there are about ten mangers in there for lambs and calves.

So I went up this rickety old ladder where they put the rest of the sacks.

It was pretty dark. I thought maybe I'd holler for Bette Davis and she'd show me. Then I thought, if she's high up she can't jump down without breaking her corny feet. And she never speaks or barks. But never.

I mooched around this top layer for ages. Goodness! I thought, Jesus is pretty well hid; in fact to tell the truth I couldn't find anything that looked like Him or Bette Davis.

'Bette Davis!' I said sternly and pretty loud. 'Hey you, Bette Davis, where are you?'

Mostly you don't hear anything, but pretty soon this white sort of stoat with long hair usually appears from under *something*; but there wasn't anything.

Then I got pretty clever. I reckoned out that maybe He never was in this part of the barn. Maybe He was in the oast – a sort of round, caplike building. Well, the bottom half is a kind of half-covered yard for the older calves, and there's another of these ladders and a *very* small door, and when you've crawled in there's a floor where the apples are stored.

I thought maybe I'd try that. No one ever goes there but Cookie because she stores these apples.

I went in. It's pretty disgusting, because you have to walk through all this cow stuff, but with my wellingtons on I didn't care so much. I climbed up the ladder and pushed the trap-door over and crawled in.

It smelt of apples. Quite a good smell, and there were still quite a lot of apples still in there, all wrinkled and beastly, like Mrs Wiggins' face. She sings in the choir. Don't ask me why. They do say she doesn't like to hear anyone else singing, so she jams these ear plugs in, and everyone has a ghastly time trying to keep up with her. But she doesn't smell of apples.

It was darker than ever in here. I had to move slowly, as I hate cracking my shins on old boxes and bits of wire.

There's only one small window, and a tiny bit of light which gets in through the top of the oast, where it used to go round in the days when they dried hops up here. It took me ages to get accustomed to the light. It did really.

It was quite still. No noise at all. Only these old rooks outside in the trees. I was getting hungry. In a moment Father would blow that bugle; and it'll mean steak and kidney.

I peered about. Not a thing could I see. True, there was a fair amount of straw about, and I *could* have picked about in it but I didn't want to. And, anyway, they said *manger*! There certainly wasn't a manger up here.

I went down again. Down this ladder.

Then I remembered.

On the other side of the covered yard was a tiny sort of place that nobody used any more. We had a pony in it once, but it was so small she couldn't lie down or turn round, and we had to get her out, the vet said. In there, there was a manger. I remember one Christmas Swallow made it into a crib, and stuck a few cobwebby angels around the place, and one of her old dolls was supposed to be the Baby. It didn't last long, because the same night one of these cats had some kittens on top of the Baby and we lost heart.

I went there immediately.

This small door is off its hinges and you have to push like crazy to get into the place, then you go in with such a rush you knock your head on the opposite wall.

I knew the form and I just sort of leaned and scrabbled through.

The manger was loaded, but loaded, with hay. It didn't look as if there was anything in there either. But I saw a bit of cake on the floor, and I knew I was off to the races.

I pulled the door behind me. It was fairly dark in here too. Well, honestly it was dark everywhere because of the fog.

I got hold of a handful of hay and pulled it off.

I knew I was on to a good thing because Bette Davis' two eyes and nose gleamed at me like currants out of the whiteness of her fur. But she didn't move. Not at all.

She was lying on somebody's chest.

It was all black in there, so I couldn't see anything much. But I could make out a sort of blurry face and eyes.

Then the face moved and I saw teeth, and knew He was smiling.

'Hullo,' He said. 'Are you another of them?'

'I s'pose you could say I was.'

He must have been awfully cramped up in the manger.

'How are you?' I asked Him, kind of politely.

'My foot's gone to sleep,' He said. I liked His voice, I did really. Sort of – well, friendly.

'Are you Jesus?' I asked Him.

'I'm not allowed to say,' He answered.

I saw the comics on the floor.

'I think it's time Bette Davis spent a penny,' I told Him. 'She has to use the comics.'

'Of course,' and He handed her to me. 'She's a nice little dog. I was glad of her company.'

'What have you been doing?' He asked me after I'd put her down and she'd obliged.

'Well, sitting on the swing and thinking really. I got my knickers a bit wet.'

'Must take care,' was all He said.

I looked down at Him. Now I could see Him better. He looked a bit ragged. Tired too.

'How did you get here?' I asked Him.

'Walked. Walked and walked and walked . . .'

'Did you come from Heaven?'

'In the beginning—'

'And you've walked ever since?'

He sighed and closed His eyes. The thought of it must have exhausted Him. He seemed to be asleep after that; and, anyway, I heard this bugle and thought I'd better go.

I put Bette Davis back on his chest, but He didn't open His eyes, so I squished my way out again and tied the door up.

As I went through the fog up to the house I thought pretty deeply. Admittedly I couldn't see anything in there, admittedly I liked His voice; and when you can only hear people you *do* get an idea of their faces. But with Him I couldn't get a face at all. And if He'd had on a policeman's helmet I couldn't have seen it.

How could He *bear* to be scrunched up in that manger! Well, He just must be dead tired, that's all . . . P'raps when He'd slept a bit and sat up we'd get a better idea.

As I got to the door I saw Mrs Gibbs' taxi. I suddenly remembered! Granny was coming to lunch. I'd ask her a few questions about Jesus. *She* should know.

Granny comes quite often. She mostly gardens, and always, but always, she has this tail of her camiknickers hanging down below her skirt. This embarrasses Poor Baby like crazy. Once he got sent to bed for the day because he tied it to a rose tree and she couldn't get up. It killed me.

'Hullo, Granny!'

'How are you, my darling?'

'Preoccupied,' I said straight away.

'Oh – with what?' She was looking at my jeans and not in the least interested.

'You shouldn't be wearing summer trousers in this weather. Where are the corduroys I gave you?'

'Oh – about—'

She and Mrs Gibbs were struggling with this basket thing she calls a suitcase, with no handle.

'Thank you, Mrs Gibbs. Six o'clock.'

'Six o'clock,' Mrs Gibbs answered. Sounded like some silly password. Then she drove away.

'Granny,' I said suddenly, 'if you saw Jesus what would you expect Him to look like?'

She paused, and dug at one of the bulbs with her umbrella.

'These should have been replaced after that hard frost.'

'What would you, Granny?'

'What would I what?'

'Expect Jesus to look like?'

'Oh, beautiful. Just beautiful.'

'How, beautiful?'

'Calm, and quiet, with lovely serene blue eyes, and He'd just stand there and say, "Woman, what wouldst thou?"'

'And what wouldst thou?'

'I should fall on my knees and say – oh dear, I've forgotten the Hebrew—'

'Why would you say that?'

'Master . . . I should say . . . Master.'

'How d'you think He's dressed?'

She looked at me intently and stuck this old case on the step. She looked very interested. She took off her hat.

'Now you come to ask me, child, I don't know. But He *is* coming again, so I may as well start thinking about how He'll be dressed.'

She was jamming a rusty old hatpin into this floppy hat and it wouldn't go.

'Give it to me,' I said. I like those jobs.

'Mind your fingers, dear.'

She took in a deep breath and inhaled all this fog.

'He will come again. P'raps as an ordinary man, like any one of us. It's up to us all, Brat, you and Swallow and Merlin, to recognise Him when He comes.'

'You don't need to worry about that,' I said, smiling to myself.

'Not trailing clouds of glory this time, but as an ordinary man.'

'I'd rather like the clouds of glory.'

'They'll be there, my dear, they'll be there, but our eyes are too dim to see glory.'

She took my hair ribbon off and started tidying up this lousy pony tail I have to wear.

'Now why did you ask me a thing like that, darling?

It's very interesting, because as I came up the drive I was thinking.'

'About what?'

'What an irreligious people we have become, and what God would say if He were suddenly to come back.'

'Not God, Granny, Jesus; we can't have them both. Someone's got to stick around and do something.'

'Where are the others?'

By now she'd got a whole lot of tight hairs in my neck. It was murder, it was really.

'Aioutch,' I hissed.

'Oh dear, your accents. Ouch, not aioutch! Now give me a hand with my Hong Kong basket.'

'Why is it a Hong Kong basket?'

'Because, dear, it came from Hong Kong.'

Just then this bugle blared out of the window in our ears.

'Slim!' yelled my grandmother.

Slim – that's my father. Everyone calls him Slim. But to my mind he's not slim at all. I mean, not like Poor Baby. He's just a skelington, that's all.

At lunch everyone did a lot of talking, so we three didn't have to. Didn't *have* to! We'd have been shut up if we'd tried.

There was Granny and old Violet. She's a particularly corny dame who comes for weekends. She wears her lipstick like a moustache and has one of those swollen voices.

There was also this actor. He didn't seem to have any name, only old Cocky. He's pretty corny, too.

'Your brother's hair is red, why isn't yours?' he asked all of a sudden. Silly really. How the hell do I know . . . ?

'Her hair is grey,' Poor Baby said. I s'pose it is too.

'It's very pretty when it's clean,' Granny said, rather pompously, I thought.

Violet was lashing into this red wine a bit, and, what's more, not leaving any dregs. This depressed me because afterwards when they're all having coffee we go round and finish off the dregs. It makes a nice afternoon.

When they'd gone Swallow went and stood by the fire.

'Did you see Him?'

I nodded. I had a huge piece of apple in my mouth.

'What did He say?'

'Said His foot had gone to sleep, then He went to sleep Himself,' I answered.

'Now look. This is to be a strict secret. Not a word to a soul.'

Swallow looked anxious.

'Why not? Everyone's got to know Jesus is back,' I said.

'All in good time. When He's not so tired.'

'Did He *say* He was Jesus. I mean, how did you *know*?' I hammered on.

'Well, not exactly, but I was in there, you see, and I heard a sound and opened the door; there He was, and He said "Knock on the door and it shall be opened to you".'

Poor Baby was smoking peacefully inside the fireplace and blowing it up the chimney.

'Well, that's enough, isn't it? I mean, *right* on the front of my Prayer Book there's that very picture and those very words.'

'Dressed right? . . . long things, and a lantern?' I was suspicious.

'Too dark to see. He was limping. I told Elizabeth, and *she* said it was *Him*.'

Actually Elizabeth remembers Him before she was born. In Heaven, as a matter of fact. She said He always walked around with a limp, and was very sweet to the children, but His mother! She said she was pretty irritable.

'Tell Brat the rest of it, though. *This* will get you.'

Poor Baby looked very profound.

I looked expectant. I needed something to get me. I did really. Up to now, between you and me, I'd been, on the whole, a bit disappointed.

'Well?' I looked round.

'Nail marks.' Swallow's eyes were nearly falling onto the fur rug.

Poor Baby blew the smoke through his nose.

'Nail marks!'

'Where?' This was getting better.

'Where d'you think?'

'Feet? . . . Hands? . . .'

'Feet.'

'Miss D. says it wasn't true. She says they were ropes,' I said.

'She doesn't know what she's talking about. I mean, *look* at that stained-glass window over Lady Pridham. All of them had nails. All of them. Thieves and all. I should say thousands of them . . . Corks! Makes me sweat to think of it.' Poor Baby made a face and held his stomach.

'That's because you inhale too deeply. You better cut smoking out.' Swallow tossed the words at him.

'In His feet, eh? Well, I give up!' I *did* too.

I remembered Granny saying that when He came it would be like an ordinary man. (I must ask Granny a few more things.)

A ghastly thought struck me! If I was a bit of a disbeliever it must mean I'm in a worse way than the others. Badder, I mean. This shook me, but *shook* me.

'What're we going to do about *Him* now?' I asked sort of respectful.

'As soon as the milking starts we'll take him some more food and drink, and blankets—'

'Isn't that manger too small?' I asked. I was full of concern, I was really.

'No. He's not all that big a man, you know.'

'Ah, how sweet.'

Don't know why I said that, but I did.

When we went back into the barn He was still asleep, so was Bette Davis. I was worried about her. I mean, she'd used her paper, but she hadn't had a chance to do anything else. I thought she ought to take a run and said so.

I shoved her outside by the dairy. She looked pretty peeved really.

Then I went back.

Swallow was looking downright worried. This Jesus was *still* asleep.

'Know something?' she said, looking at Poor Baby and me.

'No,' we said both together.

'I think He's ill. I think He's terribly ill. I'll go further, I think He has a temperature. Maybe pneumonia!'

'What about telling the vet?' Poor Baby suggested. 'He's here today.'

'We mustn't tell anyone. Not even the doctor, or the Vicar or Edward or Father or anyone.' Swallow was waving her hands about like she was excited.

'Why not?' I asked. 'If it's Jesus come back, the whole world has got to know pretty soon. You can't keep Him stuck up in this old manger, you can't really.'

'He asked me not to.' Her voice was a whisper.

'Did He? What did He say, then?' Poor Baby had got his behind stuck in a bucket.

'He said this: "Don't tell them," He said; "not till I've got on my feet."'

'What an odd type of thing to say. I mean, He can get onto His feet whenever He wants to, can't He? Anyone can.' *Honestly* – I thought that odd, I did really.

'Look at Him!' Swallow was getting a bit het up. 'He's dead ill and we've got to get Him right. Just us. Damn it, He can't *receive* wise men and shepherds and members of parliament like this, can He? I mean, use your sense.'

I had to agree.

'First we want a temperature. Poor Baby, you look in Cookie's work basket, and if there isn't one there look in Granny's Hong Kong basket or Violet's make-up box.'

'I think that's a girl's job, I do honestly.' He was still stuck in the bucket and adoring it.

'All right, I'll go,' I said, and I went.

It was quite easy to find it, it was on the sink in the kitchen. Cookie had been taking her own all day and was furious that it was normal.

I saw them all in the drive, Father and old Violet and this actor, old Cocky. Not Granny, of course; she'd gone to bed, she always does after lunch. Don't ask me why.

'Any of you coming shooting?' Father asked me.

'Afraid not today, we're a bit busy,' I said avoidingly.

They all laughed for some reason and went on to the kale field.

I took a couple of rugs out of the cars in the garage, and then I went back to the old barn.

Swallow was bending over the manger. Bette Davis had got back in somehow or other and was on her comics.

'He's talking in His sleep. Listen,' Swallow said. 'Or has he got Dee Tees?'

'What's that?' Poor Baby was half out of the bucket.

'It's what people get when they have a very high temperature,' Swallow told us.

I shook the temperature like hell before I gave it to her. I knew you had to do this, don't know why, but Cookie always does. Then I gave it to Swallow and she shoved it into His mouth.

'It's got to be under His tongue,' I told her. 'That's where Cookie has it.'

'P'raps He'll get Cookie's disease,' said Poor Baby. 'I bet these glass tubes carry germs like anything.'

Swallow didn't answer. She was so busy getting it into His mouth.

We all stood waiting. Not moving even, while Swallow counted to ninety. You have to; you see, it says a minute and a half on the temperature.

Well, then she got it out. After a struggle, mind you. His teeth had got clamped down on it.

Well, it was too dark to read it, so we all trooped outside to hear the news. It took her ages, but ages, to read the ruddy thing, and if you've tried you'll know what I mean.

When she did her eyebrows jumped up into her hair.

'It's 200!' she croaked.

'That's the record,' Poor Baby said. He was out of the bucket by now.

'It just can't be!' she sort of moaned. 'He'll die, that's all, and the world will never know.'

'Besides, how do you get rid of a dead body?' Poor Baby was very practical.

'Don't be disgusting.' I was quite cross. Actually, it was because I thought of the *Daily Mirror* or something catching us and saying we did it.

'There's only one thing: ask Edward to read it. He knows. We can always say we put it in water. Don't, for heaven's sake, say it's any of us or we'll be put to bed.' I was rather pleased with my idea.

So was Swallow.

She went straight into the dairy. Edward was hosing the floor before the cows came in. You have to.

'How do you tell a temperature, Edward?' she asked, all innocent.

'Come here and let me feel your head,' he said. Really!

'No, I've got the temperature with me,' she said. 'It looks like 200 – could that be right?'

'If it is, you're better in bed in a dark room,' and he swished on with this water.

She held it out to him.

'Look, and tell me.'

He stopped and wiped his hands on his trousers. Then he took it. He was nearly as long about reading it as we were.

'One-o-one,' he said and gave it back.

'One-o-one?' Swallow sort of muttered. 'What's that mean?'

'One hundred and one,' he said.

'Oh, good.' Swallow looked relieved.

We moved off.

'Hey,' he shouted, 'whose temp. is it?'

'It's no one's,' said Poor Baby. 'We stuck it under the tap.'

'You'll break it if you go on like that,' he said and went back to his hosing.

We got back into this place without anyone seeing us.

'I knew it,' said Swallow. 'He's got Dee Tees.'

We stood silent – looking down at Jesus. He was muttering, all right.

'God of battles, steel thy soldiers' hearts.' That's what He said!

'That's out of the Bible all right,' Poor Baby said. 'That clinches it for me.'

Swallow turned on him.

'You and Brat are unbelievers!' she said. 'Only me and Elizabeth believe, that's why He came to us. He only will come to believers. It says so in the Bible.'

This shook me. Tell you the truth, I was a teeny bit of an unbeliever, even now. It just didn't tally with my idea of Jesus, that's all.

He was on again.

'Oh . . . oh . . . oh . . .' He kept on saying 'agony'.

We felt concerned, we did really. I mean, grown-ups don't talk to you like this. They don't really.

'I don't think we should listen,' I said suddenly, and I meant it.

'Let's put these car rugs over Him and go away.'

'Certainly not,' Swallow said. 'He's ill, and we've got to look after Him.'

She put the rugs all over Him, and got some water out of the drinking thing with her hankie and washed His face.

I began to wonder what was going to be the end of all this. I mean, I could see Him being here for ever under strict secrecy, and having to remember about washing His face and hands and feeding Him and all that. Well, goodness, it would be like having those old guinea-pigs back. Such a bind really.

'Suppose He's an enemy really and goes out and sows tares among the wheat—' I said.

I was getting into Bible jargon now.

'It's no use you being so septical, Brat; it's no use. You got that thought out of the Bible, I know. But I can answer that one. Maybe He'll sow the good seed, and the Bible says, "He that soweth the good seed is the Son of Man".'

And it does too.

All afternoon really we messed about making Him comfortable. At least Swallow did it, really. We two were just there, in case – and keeping our ears open.

The others came back from shooting, with some old pheasants and rabbits hanging from their waists. I had to put them in the shed where we keep hams and bits of pigs. I hate that place, I do really. I mean, these pheasants. They're so beautiful when they're flying about, and d'you know when they get dead the colour goes out of their feathers. And all that stuff Granny gives me about being dead. 'It's leaving your overcoat behind,' she said. 'The real *you*, the soul of you, just goes to Heaven.' If that's true, why do people make so much fuss about these 'overcoats'? All these funerals and crying, like old Mrs

Dodd when Bert got took. Flowers and people crying, and solemn men in high black hats whispering and shoving you out of the way.

No one, but no one, cries over the pheasants.

They just sit down and eat them.

S'pose this man in there dies? What about that? All this secrecy. We'd have to go out at night and dig a hole on the dump. It's all too awful. I've a good mind to sneak. I have really.

At tea-time Granny suddenly said, 'You children are very silent. What have you been up to?'

If you're silent you've always been *up* to something. You're never allowed to be alone with your thoughts.

'We're alone with our thoughts,' I said.

'Sounds like a guilty conscience,' Violet said.

Really!

We didn't want to watch this old television. It's awful, anyway, except for the play about hospitals, and that was Mondays. We didn't even want to play poker, and Poor Baby makes a packet every time he plays. In fact they *begged* him.

'*Please*, Poor Baby, it'd make a good school.'

He was watching Swallow. He knew she was going to be off to the barn, and he wanted to go too.

'Where's Bette Davis?' Granny asked. 'I haven't seen her all day.'

'She's gone hunting,' Swallow said, cramming her mouth with bun.

'She'll get lost down a rabbit-hole,' Granny warned.

'She always gets out again,' Poor Baby told her, 'on account of the rabbits think she's a ferret, anyway.'

'Well, there certainly is an air of gloom about this

evening. Come on, who's done something they shouldn't have?'

Makes you sick, really it does.

'Think I'll take a small saunter,' Swallow said, and eyed us two sharply.

'Same here,' we both said and followed her out.

We heard those grown-ups laughing as we went.

'They'll laugh the other side of their faces when they find out we've got Jesus in the barn,' Swallow said majestically.

By now we were pretty well organised in our minds. We had a hurricane lamp (well, you had to, it was pitch in there), also a paraffin stove. I was particularly glad about the latter. *I'm* absolutely crazy about that smell. Swallow says it goes back to pre-birth in my case.

Oh yes, and I had my bottle of Alka-Seltzers. Actually, it's not mine, to be truthful. It's Cookie's. It's the one she hits her back with. I often wonder if she notices it getting lighter. I have a couple every day. She never takes them, she says.

We had toast and cake and things we'd pinched from tea, and we got some milk from the dairy before they had finished milking.

It was getting to be twilight. Coupled with the fog, it made it pretty ghostly.

When we got into the barn, you wouldn't believe it, but the place was stuffed with these doves we have. They were stuck up all over the place in the roof.

'Good Lord, look at the doves!' Poor Baby said. 'What the heck are they doing in here instead of their houses?'

'It's because it's Holy Ground and they know it. Don't you know what doves are supposed to be?'

'They can't *all* be the Holy Ghost,' Poor Baby said. That killed me.

He was still lying in the same position. In fact so far I hadn't seen Him shift, and that was about six hours. No kidding, He was ill all right.

Swallow said to hold up His head while she poured in some milk, and I did. It was a huge head, and very heavy, but I managed with a bit of a struggle. The milk dribbled out of His mouth like it does when you feed a calf, but I think some went in all right.

His head was hotter than ever, and sort of wet.

'He's sweating,' I said to Swallow, and she nodded.

Poor Baby stared at Him.

'Say something, if it's only goodbye,' he said suddenly.

Of course that's a grown-up joke he'd heard, but it wasn't very good taste in view of the circumstances, and I told him so.

'Well, it's all taking so long,' he complained.

'When a person is ill, they're ill,' Swallow said. 'You just have to have patience, like we all did when you had earache.'

'D'you think He's got earache?' Poor Baby asked. 'He did say something about agony.'

'That's right, He did,' I nudged Swallow.

Just at this moment He opened His eyes.

'Have you got earache?' I asked Him.

He took a great breath and closed His eyes again

'He's got earache,' I said.

'I'll get some hot oil.' Poor Baby was almost out of the door before he'd said it.

We didn't stop him going.

Well, we waited for ages for this oil. Nothing happened

in the barn at all. The hurricane lamp made us into funny shapes and the doves woke up and tried to get at the cake. Stanley (he's the father of them all – I mean he marries the lot) literally wrenched it away from me.

I didn't think the doves were being too holy.

No sign of this boy with the oil.

'Bet he had second thoughts about poker,' I said to Swallow.

He's mad, but mad, on this poker – and lucky. He always has a full house or fours or something, and it's the same when he throws dice.

'Bet you anything,' I said, 'he's caught them playing poker and had a quick hand.'

'He won't stay long,' Swallow reminded me. 'It's Sunday and he can't play for money.'

This was true.

A moment later he was back, with a bottle of salad oil. It was frozen absolutely solid, and we had to put it on the paraffin stove.

'Bet you had a hand of poker,' I said to him.

'Correct.' The salad oil was beginning to melt. 'I brought my fountain-pen filler too.'

That was fairly thoughtful.

Well, after a while it had melted enough to get some in the fountain-pen filler, and Swallow turned Jesus' head and first squirted some in one ear, and then the other.

He *was* in a mess. Milk all over His face and salad oil all in His ears and hair.

Still, if it did the trick . . .

Suddenly we heard a sound!

People!

We all looked at each other, scared as hell.

Swallow pushed some of this hay up all over Him and we stood about warming our hands. I even got hold of old Stanley and literally stuffed him with cake.

The door started to heave open.

Murder!

It was Elizabeth. We all breathed out heavily with relief.

'Look out,' she said. 'That Amos Nodge is in the dairy.'

You wouldn't like Amos Nodge. I don't much. He has a Nanny, and the first time I met him was at some lousy party. He came up to me and said, 'My Nanny says I can play with you if you wipe your nose.'

Well, I didn't, and he didn't. He's older now, but I wouldn't trust him far. He still has a Nanny, even though he's nine.

'Another thing,' said Elizabeth, 'so is Crikky and Susan.'

Crikky and Susan are Edward's children. They're all right. Trouble was they know this place and they might come in and, if they do, so does old Nodge. That Nanny would have it round the pubs about Jesus in no time.

There was another noise. A grown-up's sort of breathing noise. This was *it* – now we'd had it in a big way.

Poor Baby was pretty sharp. He went through the door and we heard him talk to someone.

'What you doing with that calf, Eric?' we heard him say.

'She's sick. Want to put her in the small barn.'

The small barn! That's *here*!

I had goose pimples all over me.

'Why?' asked Poor Baby outside the door.

'Nice and warm in there,' Eric answered.

'Well, we're playing mothers and fathers in here,' Poor Baby said, very cleverly I thought. 'But if she *must* come in, I'll take her.'

'You ain't got one of them kerosene things in there, have you?' Eric asked.

'No,' said Poor Baby, which was true because it was paraffin.

'Think you can manage?' Eric asked. S'pose he was thinking of his tea.

'Brat will help,' I heard Poor Baby reply.

Next minute this struggling boy emerged with a maniacal calf.

Five days old it was, and fighting like crazy.

Well, I did help. It was heavy as hell, and its sticking-out hooves trampled all over my bedroom slippers. It damn near knocked the paraffin thing over too, but after what seemed hours to me Poor Baby, Elizabeth and I got it jammed in a corner and tied it up.

I'd seen this one being born. Amazing really.

Swallow never looked up from the manger once. That gives you an idea of her concentration powers.

Well, there we all were in this teeny place – Jesus and the calf, and all these doves, not to mention us four.

'You better go and get its food,' I said to Poor Baby, 'otherwise we'll have Eric in here again.'

He went. The worst of it was, when he came back with this bucket of milk Crikky and Susan were behind him.

We were appalled.

Swallow had all this hay on top of Jesus, and she sat on the manger swinging her feet, so they didn't see anything.

'What you doin'?' Crikky asked.

'Playin',' Elizabeth said straight away.

'Can we play?' Susan asked.

'It's rather a sophisticated game,' I said.

'Yes, Biblical,' Elizabeth added.

They looked confused.

'Can't you explain it, then?' Crikky asked.

We had to keep our beads on him. He's nine and pretty sharp.

'Take too long, it would really,' Poor Baby said, while he was cramming this calf's face into the milk bucket.

'We can watch then, can't we, Crik?' Susan said, grinning.

'It's nothing to watch. It's just lofty words, that's all,' Poor Baby said. He was covered with milk too by now.

'Like what?' asked Crikky.

'Like Ameeba,' Poor Baby answered.

'What's that, for instance?' Crikky demanded.

'It's what some people say Bette Davis looks like, if you want to know,' I said slowly, remembering old Cocky.

'Oh.'

Everyone stood about and said nothing and just stared at each other after that. The time was ticking away, and I thought, This Jesus is suffocating under the hay.

Then He moved. Turned right over on His side, pulling all the rugs and hay with Him. You could see the back of His head quite clearly. You could really.

Crikky and Susan looked at Him.

'Who you got in the manger then?' he asked.

'A friend,' said Swallow.

'Yes, a weekend friend,' added Poor Baby. 'He's playing this game with us, this sophisticated game.'

I was hot as hell in there. This paraffin stove and the

41

hurricane lamp, and all these people and calves, and the doves breathing . . . it killed me.

'You all look funny to me,' Crikky said after a bit. 'You look as if you're all doing something you shouldn't. Think I'll tell Dad.'

This was the pay-off. Dangerous stuff. The last thing we wanted.

Swallow made up her mind.

'Can you two keep a secret? A really *big secret*?'

'Try us,' Crikky said.

'You've got to hold up your hand and do the "See this wet" routine,' Swallow said. She looked awfully solemn.

They held up their hands and said after her:

> 'See this wet,
> See this dry,
> Cross my heart if I tell a lie.'

'Well?' said Crikky.

Susan got out a bag of bull's-eyes, and we all had one.

'This is a great and fabulous secret, known to none but those within these walls. You have to join a society to be allowed to know the secret, and all who know must swear on their dying oath never to divulge.'

'Is it Brat's society? Because we belong to that already,' Susan said.

(I must tell you here and now, my society is U.S.H. . . . that means Society against the Unrightful Slaughter of Horses. That's what she was meaning.)

'No,' said Swallow, 'something of even greater importance.'

Well, I s'pose she's right.

'Will you absolutely swear?' Swallow demanded.

'We've done it, haven't we, with all that "See this wet"?'

I could see Crikky was impatient to know.

'If you ever breathe a word something ghastly will happen to you,' Poor Baby said, and Swallow nodded.

'Well, we do swear, don't we, Sue? We're jolly good at keeping secrets. There's a lot goes on in our house we never tell on . . . never will.'

'All right,' said Swallow, 'we trust you implicit.'

Then she got off the manger and pulled back the hay and things.

They went nearer and stared down at the man in the manger. He was still asleep, and you could see the oil on His face shining in the light. Some of the toast was in there with Him, and Stanley was at it.

'Who is it, then? What's so secret about some feller sleeping in a manger?' Crikky seemed madly disappointed.

'*Ah!*' said Swallow. 'But *what* feller? Who *is* it?'

'How should I know?' Crikky said, sort of sharp. 'I don't know your weekend guests, do I?'

'Well, I'll tell you. Always remembering your vow to the society.'

They looked at her expectantly. She couldn't bring herself to say it. She pointed at the dove eating the toast.

'What does that picture put you in mind of?' she asked.

'That's old Stanley, that's who that puts me in mind of.' Crikky was getting fed-up, I could see that.

'A dove . . . a holy dove,' Swallow said.

'I tell you it's old Stanley. I'd know him anywhere.'

'He may be old Stanley. For years we've all known him as old Stanley. But in fact, unbeknownst to us, he is a holy dove, and we're very privileged to have him with us.'

'Rotten secret,' Susan said, and put away her bag of bull's-eyes.

'Well, anyway,' said Crikky, 'who is this feller all squeezed up in the manger?'

'That's Jesus!' Swallow said it triumphantly but quietly.

'Jesus!' Crikky was thunderstruck. I could see that.

'Jesus,' said Poor Baby. 'Just Jesus, that's all.'

Crikky didn't know what to say. He didn't really.

'It isn't,' said Susan. Rather rudely, I thought.

'We have proof,' I said sternly. Though actually we hadn't much.

'Has Dad and them others seen Him?' Crikky asked.

'Of course not. We are the privileged few so far. They will, of course, in time and so will the whole world. Thousands and thousands of people will pour into this farm pretty soon.'

'Like Butlins?' asked Susan. She'd just heard of Butlins, to tell you the truth, because her big brother was going there for his summer holidays.

'Like Butlins,' agreed Swallow, half-heartedly.

Crikky sat down by the calf. He looked shattered. He did really.

'How d'you know it's Him?' he asked.

'He told us; didn't He, Elizabeth?' Swallow turned to Elizabeth and she nodded furiously.

'When and how?' Crikky pressed on.

Elizabeth took up the story. Her eyes were purple again and her face was black in the shadows.

'Me'n Swallow was in here messing about. There was a sort of knock on the door, an' Swallow opened it. He stood there smilin' at us and said, "Knock on the door and it shall be opened unto you"—an' *she* said "Who are you?" and He stood staring round this place, not answerin' at once, and then suddenly He said, rather loud: "*Jesus!*" just like that . . .'

She'd said it all in one breath and had to stop, so Swallow went on:

'His legs were all cut and His boots and socks crammed with mud, and He kind of lurched – you know how drunk people do—'

'P'raps He *was* drunk . . .'

I could see Crikky was an unbeliever.

'He wasn't at all! He toppled over to that manger and half fell in; I asked Him if I should get someone, and He said, "Don't tell them till I've recovered".'

'Tell them what?' I was glad to see Susan get out her bag of bull's-eyes again.

'That He was Jesus, of course,' Swallow said, a bit annoyed.

'Know something?' said Crikky. 'I've got to have a great ruddy miracle before I'm going to believe.'

That's what I'd felt, but I hadn't said it.

'You will, you see if you don't. He's ill, too ill to talk yet, He's been asleep for six hours, in the *daytime*! He's got a one-o-one temperature. Give the man a chance!'

'All right,' said Crikky agreeably, 'I will.'

Swallow suddenly had another thought.

'And another thing, just let me show you something.'

She went over to the manger and struggled with Jesus till she had hold of both feet.

'*Look!*' she said.

We all crowded round and looked.

In the centre of both feet were holes.

All of a sudden I was convinced. I hadn't seen them before.

Crikky stared.

'You mean? . . . you mean . . . ?' He couldn't go on, he couldn't really.

'I *do* mean,' said Swallow.

'Cor!' said Crikky.

I could see we had him at last.

He stood staring at us and then back at the man. His face went all thoughtful. Well, sloppy really.

'The manger . . . and doves . . . and a newborn calf . . . sweet, isn't it?'

Swallow looked so pleased.

'So you see, Crik, not a word, not yet, not till He's better and can tell us what He wants us to do. Don't you agree?'

Crik nodded.

Susan passed round the bull's-eyes.

'Suppose . . . just suppose, the grown-ups don't believe, s'pose they try and take Him away . . . after all, they did last time.' He spoke slowly and with horror, I thought.

This hadn't crossed our minds, but we had to admit the possibility. It was rather awful.

'After all, the grown-ups crucified Him, didn't they?' Crikky asked, and we had to agree.

'I know,' said Swallow. 'There's hundreds of children round here, and every child knows other children. We can have a gigantic meeting, we can tell all of them, swear them all to secrecy. Bring them a few at a time, like a pilgrimage, to see Him and hear His words. Secretly we can spread the news to children all over the country, so that the first people to know Jesus has come back will be the children, *and* – if the grown-ups try to take Him away again we'll defend Him. Hundreds of us.'

'Good show,' said Poor Baby.

We all agreed. We all shook hands, and dipped our fingers in blood. Actually it was Elizabeth's blood – a cut on her knee which had healed. She scratched it open again.

Then Crikky said he had to go to tea, and they went. I was sorry because of the bull's-eyes, but I do agree everything must seem ordinary.

Jesus was *still* asleep!

We agreed to go to the nursery and get to bed early, then when everyone was asleep we'd come back.

'We could use my alarum,' Swallow said.

We put out the lights, collected up Bette Davis and went.

When Cookie came to the nursery to tell us it was bed-time she asked us what we were reading.

'Revelations,' I said. Because we were.

47

Three

It was two o'clock when my alarum went off. Everybody calls it an alarum. Don't ask me why. I had to fling myself on it and get it into the bed with me in case anyone woke up and thought it was that old telephone.

The other two took a lot of waking. I wished they'd all had alarums, but the noise would have been tremendous.

We pulled on our trousers over our pyjamas, like Father does when he goes out milking, shoved socks on and then crawled like snails down these stairs with the matting on them.

It's not too easy to open the kitchen door without a click, but we made it. It isn't easy, as that door has just about the noisiest click any door ever had; and Cookie goes by that click. Any other time she'd have been out of her room like a stoat, but this night there weren't any groanings or curses from her room, so we went on out.

The whole countryside was lit up with moonlight, and smelled sweet, like spring was coming. We had to admit it was pretty good.

We ran into one or two of these cats pawing round the place, and Poor Baby stood on one of them. It let off a hell of a piercing yell, and we had to lean back against the wall.

Lucky for us we looked up at Violet's window without going any farther. She was there leaning out and staring around. She has to do this because of her hangover. She needs air.

Well, we just had to go the long way round. We didn't have Bette Davis with us, because she sleeps in the bath, and, to tell you the truth, I'd forgotten about her.

Oddly enough, I was sweating. I can't tell you why; I told Poor Baby, and he said he was too. We all tailed along after Swallow, who was skimming a bit, but when we got to the barn door we all stopped.

We were all a bit terrified, we were honestly. Well, we'd never been on this sort of a jaunt before, and we weren't too sure what we'd find inside. I mean, He could have been dead for all we knew, and then what were we to do? I mean, you can't just go back and get into bed, knowing someone was dead in the barn.

We could hear some scratching about going on over our heads. We reckoned it was rats or bats or birds or something.

'I wish I had something comforting to eat,' Poor Baby said, and I agreed.

'There's cake and toast and stuff in there,' Swallow said; but that didn't make us feel any too good. I mean, you can't be nursing someone back to health and just go in and sit down and eat up all His cake.

We were near the swing, so I sat on it. Swings are very cheering things if you want to think.

'I think we've made a hideous mistake,' I told Swallow.

'I don't think I should have let my alarum off. I think we should all still be asleep, like everyone else.'

'Violet isn't asleep,' she reminded me, 'nor are those old cats Poor Baby trod on.'

'There's a certain amount of night life,' admitted Poor Baby; 'but my feet are cold.'

Which is not to be wondered at, as we were only in our stockings.

'Well, it's our duty to see He's all right. After all, night nurses are up all night looking after the patients, aren't they?'

I'd hate like hell to be a night nurse. I would really. I mean, there can't be anything to do but empty poes and things. This reminded me I wanted to spend a penny. So I did. Swallow was pretty angry because she said I made such a noise with it.

In the end we went in.

Just inside the door were these hurricane lamps, so we lit one with Poor Baby's matches and crawled through the damp old barn still in our stocking feet, which were pretty cold by now.

Jesus was *still* asleep!

Well, naturally I s'pose He would be. Anyone would be in the middle of the night.

Swallow put her hand on His head. He jumped right up, and sat staring; you know, like people do when they get wakened up suddenly and don't know where they are. Except that I always know where I am, because I'm in my bedroom. But I could see it was different for Him, as He was in a strange place. Quite strange, you could say.

Well, we all stared at Him, and He at us.

He looked lousy.

His face was terrible white in the hurricane light, and His hair was all over the place.

Then suddenly He sort of grinned.

'Hullo,' He said. 'It's you again, is it?'

We said it was.

'Are you feeling better?' Swallow asked Him. 'You've been ill all day with a temperature of one-o-one, and we thought we'd better come and see what kind of a night you were having.'

'What time is it?' He asked.

'Two a.m.,' she said.

'Two a.m.?' He seemed surprised. 'You mean to say you three got out of your beds at two a.m. to see how I was?'

We nodded.

'Well, I think that's the nicest thing I ever heard of,' He said. 'No one's ever been as nice as that to me, not as long as I can remember. Three kids . . . I call that wonderful. Makes you believe in human nature again.'

He smiled at us all round, and then He held out His hand to us.

'I'd like to shake you by the hand,' He said, and did.

'Do you feel better?' Swallow asked again, and He nodded.

'I'm all right. I think I've had a chill. I must press on.'

He tried to struggle up out of the manger as if He wanted to go straight away. But Swallow stopped Him.

'Oh, you can't go yet,' she said; 'you're not well enough.'

'That's very kind of you, but I must press on,' and

He frowned a bit, as if He didn't much want to go, anyway.

'Why must you press on?' Poor Baby was messing about with these matches, dying to light up a bit of hay.

'I don't want to get you kids into trouble, do I – just because you sheltered me?' Then He laughed. 'What'll your mother say if she catches you out here at two a.m.?'

'That's all right,' I said. 'You don't have to worry on our account, you don't really. I mean, we haven't got a mother.'

'Oh, I'm sorry,' and He looked sorry too. 'I remember when I was six my mother used to cry a great deal,' He said.

'Really?' I answered. 'I wonder why?'

He shrugged His shoulders and sort of smiled.

'Probably,' Poor Baby said, 'because with all that carpentry she thought you'd hammer a finger or something.'

I s'pose He was thinking of His mother, because He didn't answer.

I was beginning to feel darn cold, I was really. My feet were like ice, and I wanted to sit down. Actually I wanted to be back in bed, so I did the next best thing and sat on the wet floor.

'You'll give yourself piles if you sit there,' He said. I got up at once.

'What's piles?' I asked. I s'pose I should have known, but I have a bit of a bird brain.

'It's what you get from sitting on cold wet stones,' He said, and I thanked Him for noticing.

'You're sweet kids, that's what you are. Why on earth should you be so good to a stranger?'

'For one thing we know who you are,' Swallow said, and she grinned.

'You do?' His voice was very quiet; I noticed this from the start.

'And we're going to look after you,' she added.

'Are you?' He wasn't smiling any more. 'Why should you want to?'

'Because I don't s'pose anyone believes in you, do they?' I asked.

He shook His head and sighed a bit.

'No—'

'Well, we do,' said Swallow, 'and very soon hundreds of us all over the country will.'

'Hundreds?' He seemed madly interested because He leaned forward suddenly, but actually He was after a bit of Stanley's left-over cake, which He ate.

'Thousands – could be,' Swallow went on.

She looked at us and we nodded. To tell the truth there were only six of us, but by the time He needed them there *would* be more.

'Thousands? . . . of people?' He wasn't after the cake now. There was a bit in the corner. I saw Poor Baby eyeing it. Could have done with it myself.

'Not *people*!' Swallow replied. 'Children.'

'Honestly?' He seemed a bit pleased. 'How's that? How do they know about me? Is it in the papers?'

'We haven't seen any papers,' Poor Baby told Him. He was after this bit of cake and he fell in the manger.

Jesus helped him out, and gave him the cake.

'How do you know who I am?' He asked me.

'Well, Swallow and Elizabeth told me,' and that was true.

'Who told Swallow and Elizabeth?' He kept on at me.

'You did yourself. You said your name when you came in here. Of course, you might not have meant to, as you were a bit sick with this one-o-one temperature. But there you are, you did.'

'And you haven't told anyone else?'

'Of course not,' Swallow said, 'because you asked me not to. "Don't tell them till I've recovered" – that's what you said. A few of us kids know, but you're perfectly safe with us.'

'I bet I am,' He said and grinned all over His face. 'I bet there's more of the milk of human kindness in kids than there is in anyone.'

He ruffled up Poor Baby's hair.

'I shall never forget you kids. When I'm lonely or sick or scared, and I am scared sometimes, I shall remember you kids.'

'Why don't people believe in you, then?' Poor Baby asked Him; he likes having his head scratched.

'That's a very long old story.'

'You can say that again,' Poor Baby replied. 'Just about the longest old story, that's all.'

'I shouldn't worry too much,' I told Him. 'It's these grown-ups, they don't believe in *anything*, not anything. If you tell them something quite ordinary and corny they go off into this phoney laughter. I've given them up, I have really.'

He didn't laugh.

'They don't even *do* anything much,' Poor Baby said. 'And if you go so far as to offer them a bit of gum or something, they just go "Ugh" at you. When we all grow up it'll be different.'

'Will it? I wonder. That's the tragedy, old son. When you go through that barrier, marked "The End of Childhood", you become one of them. You forget. It's sad, but you forget. The older we get, the more we forget of our decisions and plans.' He took a hold of my pony tail and pulled it. 'Know something, young lady? When you were very very tiny, one and a half maybe, you even remember things like being born, and before *that* even. Now I bet you don't remember any more!'

'No, I don't actually, but Elizabeth does, and Poor Baby used to tell us about fighting his way down a long black passage.'

He turned and looked at Poor Baby. He looked like a sort of gnome in this old light of the lamp, Poor Baby did.

'I bet you've forgotten too,' He said quietly.

'You mean, forgotten you?' Poor Baby asked Him.

'Oh, I don't think you've ever seen me in your life before,' Jesus said. 'But then again, you could have, somewhere—'

'Elizabeth says you walked with a limp. Do you still?' Swallow asked Him, sort of eager beaver.

'Yes, I do. I always will. I've got a hole right through my foot.'

'*Both* feet you mean!' Poor Baby reminded Him.

He looked quite surprised. He did really.

'That's right, both feet—'

'Must have hurt,' Poor Baby said. 'I stuck a pitchfork in my foot, that was bad enough, and I don't s'pose you had a tetnus injection, did you?'

The man in the manger shook His head. He looked very tired all of a sudden.

'Are you hungry and thirsty?' Swallow asked Him. She's very good about being social. Always remembers to ask people if they want a drink.

'I am a bit,' He admitted, 'but don't you worry, it's too late.'

'I can get some bread and milk, or some whisky and soda if you like it better,' I told Him. Anything to move around on these wet ice-cold feet.

'You haven't any shoes on,' He told me.

'That's all right,' I answered. 'Look at my feet, they're sodding. I can't even feel them.'

'Go on, Brat, get some bread.' She turned to Jesus. 'Would you like some wine?—bread and wine?—so we can make it a sort of – you know—'

This made Him laugh. Don't ask me why.

Anyway, I went.

It was freezing cold and all grey and horrid again. This old moon had given up the struggle and disappeared, and there were clouds right down to my ears.

I got back into the kitchen with no one seeing me. Old Violet had given up the unequal struggle, too, and gone back to bed.

I found the bread in the bin, and I looked under the cupboard for the wine bottle Cookie uses for sauces and soups. I saw this bottle of vinegar and nearly took it by mistake, and I thought, that's a bit near the knuckle, I thought, and I took this old dreggy bottle instead.

Hell, it was lovely and warm by the Aga. I nearly ratted and didn't go back. But I liked this man. He wasn't a phoney grown-up hollering and squawking.

I liked His quiet voice and the way He grinned. Honestly, I thought He was all right. He slayed me, He did really.

Everything was going fine, and I was on my way out again when one of these lousy cats that hang about thinking of nothing but food and mice jumped on me from the frig and knocked the top off of the dustbin.

It made the hell of a noise and I had to leg it as fast as I could in these stockings and getting stones and things in my toes.

I literally threw the bread at Jesus and elbowed the wine into the manger.

'Hey, Swallow,' I sort of hissed, 'one of those corny cats kicked the hell out of the dustbin, and Cookie is bound to be nosing about with that poker.'

Swallow doesn't waste much time, and in a second she had the hay all over the top of Him, all in the bread and everything.

'Lie still,' she whispered. 'Don't move, or munch loudly; no one will come in here, no one at all.'

Then she suddenly got hold of my arm and squeezed it till I nearly shrieked.

'What about that calf!'

'I know,' said Poor Baby. 'Eric doesn't come till five-thirty. Brat can get up again and stand around like she's anxious to help him.'

'Why not you?' I said in a deadly voice.

'Because you have the alarum,' he told me.

We could see the hay going up and down as though someone was laughing.

'Well, all right,' I said.

I don't believe I'd have done it for anyone else. I don't really.

When we finally got back to the kitchen door it was locked.

We knew Cookie had been up, but she'd gone back to bed, as all the lights were out.

We climbed up this wistaria tree to old Violet's bathroom and tiptoed to our beds.

When I got under the clothes I felt like I'd got a cold, so I took out my little Victor Inhaler and had a long sniff. Then I put this bloody alarum right for five-thirty . . .

*   *   *

I looked in on Jesus before I struggled with this calf.

'Are you okay?' I asked Him.

'Yes, I'm okay,' He said, 'but cold, terrible cold.'

I went back to the washroom and found Him another blanket. He didn't look too good to me, and I wished Swallow was with me.

It was just on five-thirty. I knew these men would be along soon for the milking, so I hung about.

Pretty soon I saw my father coming down from the house. He looked surprised to see me, he really did.

'What on earth are you doing at this time of the morning?' he asked.

'I couldn't sleep,' I told him, 'so I thought I'd come down and help with the milking, or the calves, or *something*,' I said.

'That's very considerate. Very considerate indeed.' He seemed quite pleased in a way. 'First thing you can do is make some tea,' he said. 'I could do with a cuppa.'

Hell, I thought. *I'm* making the tea, and then Eric goes in and finds Jesus.

'Sure you want tea?' I asked. 'What about a nice drink of Alka-Seltzer?'

'No, tea,' he said and went off into the cowshed.

I was pretty peeved. I seem to have been up all night, and I kept thinking of Swallow and Poor Baby asleep in their warm beds.

Well, anyway, I went back to the kitchen and made the tea, and put on an extra cup for Jesus.

The wind was whistling down the drive and nearly blew all these damn cups over. I was fed-up, I was really. I took it into the cowshed and everyone seemed pleased enough.

'You've got a cup too many,' Dad said.

'Yes. Well, I don't know why,' I said. 'Think I'll take my cuppa outside in the air. All this smell of cow-pats kills me in the early morning, it does really.'

I got out with my cup and took it straight in to Jesus. He was thrilled.

'You're a good kid,' He said. 'That'll just about put me right. My feet are murder.'

He didn't look too good. I shoulda taken his temperature, but Swallow had it. He looked as if it had gone up to one-o-one again. But there wasn't anything I could do, so I went back into the cowshed.

Bess, one of the cows, had sat right down in the middle of everything and couldn't move. Dad and the others were staring at her and pushing and shoving.

'Mastitisis,' Edward said, and Dad hummed.

I felt sorry for her. She looked so big and bony and sort of embarrassing lying about in all the muck. But there's something about cows' fringes that is most endearing. I stroked it and said:

'Poor old girl.' I kept hearing myself saying it and couldn't stop. Maybe I was half asleep.

'I'll feed that calf,' I told Eric, and he seemed pleased, and poured the milk out into a bucket.

Well, I staggered back into the stable where Jesus and the calf were and started to feed her. He watched me all the time while He drank His tea.

'I ought to go, Brat,' He said.

'Not till Swallow says so,' I told Him. The calf's mouth was all slimy and I wasn't enjoying any part of it.

'This tea is balm in Gilead,' He said and snuggled down again under the blanket. 'I wish I could stay here forever.'

'You can if you want to,' I told Him, but He laughed and shook His head.

'I can't settle anywhere yet,' He said. 'I have to keep moving.'

'Why?' I asked Him.

'The time is not ripe' is all He said.

I don't think I've ever felt more tired. I was kind of rolling. I wished I was in bed and everything was just the same as usual. Then horrors descended on me and I realised it was Monday! In about two and a half hours this Land-Rover would be outside the door to take us to school!

'Look here,' I said, 'it's Monday, and we have to go to school. Will you be okay?'

'Hope so,' He said.

'We'll bring you food and stuff before we go, of course,' I said, 'but we don't come back till four-thirty, so you must stay hidden.'

He nodded. He didn't look too happy.

When I'd finished the calf and cleaned out the bucket I went back to the cowshed and had a cup of tea. It was strong and beastly and fitted in with my mood. I had a foul old cold by now and didn't feel too good. I got up on this cow Oona and sat on her back. She quite enjoys people on her back.

'What's all this sneezing?' Father asked me.

'I gotta cold,' I said and blew my brains out on my hanky.

'Better get something for it, or go back to bed till Cookie is up,' he said.

A sudden idea struck me. If my cold was real bad I wouldn't have to go to school and could sleep a bit and then keep my eye on Jesus! I made like it was even worse. You know, sort of hanging nose and open mouth and eyes all bleary.

'I don't think Miss D. would care for me to take this cold to school,' I told Father. 'It makes her cross when kids have colds.'

'You better see Cookie and tell her I said to stay in bed for a bit,' he said.

I was pretty pleased about this. All the same, I *did* have a cold, and I thought maybe I won't use my little Victor Inhaler and then I can be on guard.

I went in and told Cookie.

She was livid.

She hates us hanging about and not being in school. It means more cooking, and looking after people with trays and things.

'Dad said I was to take this cold to bed,' I said.

'Go on then,' she said, and pushed one of these cats out of the window.

The house was freezing and the wind was howling. I felt like hell. I like the house when old Nellie is hoovering and the fires are lit.

I got old Bette Davis out of the bath and took her in bed with me. She's very warm and comforting, but it's a bit like having a rabbit in bed with you.

I must have gone to sleep, because I woke up suddenly and there was Swallow and Poor Baby by the bed.

'What's the time?' I asked them.

'Ten o'clock,' Swallow said and looked very odd.

'Why aren't you both in school, then?' I asked.

'It's most peculiar,' Swallow said, 'but Father told us we weren't to go!'

I sat up.

'Why not?'

Swallow shook her head.

'Maybe he thinks I've got chicken-pox or something.' I felt quite thrilled at the idea and started looking for spots.

'No, it isn't that,' she said. 'We were having breakfast and Father said you had this cold and to leave you alone, and then the phone goes, and he has a long talk – you know, "Yes, yes, oh? oh? no, no" – and then he comes back to the table and says, "You two better stay home as well today."'

'Maybe Miss D. has something infectious,' I suggested.

'Anyway, I said I wasn't feeling on my sparks either,' Poor Baby said. 'In fact I didn't eat my prunes just to show.'

'It's wonderful luck,' said Swallow, 'because now we can keep our eye on you-know-who.'

'Can it be anything to do with Him?' I asked. 'I mean,

63

maybe He's created a miracle because He knew we were tired.'

Swallow shook her head again.

'No, it's just luck,' she said. 'I think maybe Poor Baby and I better go and see Him.'

'He wasn't too good at five-thirty,' I told her. 'He was freezing cold.'

'Not dead!' Poor Baby looked horrified.

'Oh no. He had some tea,' I reassured them.

When they'd gone I leaned back on the pillow and stroked Bette Davis.

I wasn't so pleased with everything now.

Here I was stuck in this bedroom with a phoney cold and they weren't going to school either. I was fed-up, I was really. My room was icy and I could hear this wind yelling round the house, and I'd read all the books on the shelf a dozen times.

I got out and called down the stairs for Cookie or Nellie. Nellie is Cookie's friend who grubs round the house with this Hoover and crawls round the baths with that pink stuff that smells nice. No one came and I was hungry, so I got out a lump of chocolate I keep among my sweaters for special occasions and had a bite of it with Bette Davis.

My nose felt all bunged up, so I had a little go with my little Victor, then I must have gone to sleep again.

There still wasn't any sign of life when I woke up, but there was a tray of stuff by the bed. The tea was cold again.

I was getting sick of cold tea, I was really. So I ate the toast and got out my dictionary and looked up 'Purpose' – 'Idea or aim kept before the mind as the end of effort.' That's what it said. I couldn't make head or tail of it, honestly I couldn't. The word below looked more interesting: 'Purpura' – 'e.g. an eruption of small purple spots, caused by extravation of blood in the skin, sometimes called the purples'.

I wondered whether to have it, and looked round for my mauve crayon, but I couldn't find it and decided against it, anyway. I was pretty sick of bed already, and this would mean more of it.

I got on my sweater and trousers and crept downstairs.

I heard Cookie talking to Granny and listened.

'No wonder she has a bad cold,' Cookie was saying. 'They were out in the early hours of the morning, the three of them. I guess she took cold.'

'Oh dear!' Granny was moaning. 'They're just growing up like wild animals.'

I wish we were, I thought. I just wish we were.

'And now this added horror. Well, thank goodness I'm here to help you, Cookie dear.'

I was hoping to hear more, but they seemed to have gone away, and when I got down to the room it was empty.

Added horror? What could Granny mean?

I took another look at my chest but I didn't see any spots, red or purpura. So I went on down to the cowshed.

There didn't seem to be anyone about, except this old dog Charlie Staircase, who was sniffing round the swing.

'Find Swallow, find Swallow,' I said encouragingly, but he cut me stone dead and went off in the other direction with his nose on the ground.

I had to find out what this added horror was. I was

beginning to get in a bit of a stew, even wondered if I had some awful disease and everyone was avoiding me.

I went into the stable.

To my surprise it was full.

Swallow, Poor Baby, Crikky, Susan, Elizabeth, Shirley, Pippa, Jeremy, Andrew, Rosanna and Jenny.

You couldn't move, you couldn't really.

'What in heck is going on?' I asked, and they all jumped.

'What in heck are you all doing not at school?' I asked.

'There isn't any school,' Shirley said. 'All of us, but all of us is away from school!'

'Has Miss D. got something, then?' I asked. Then I remembered Granny and Cookie. 'Listen,' I said to them, 'I heard Granny tell Cookie there was an "added horror".'

'That's why we aren't at school,' Jeremy said. 'But what?'

'It must be the plague, the black plague,' Pippa said, 'that's all it could be.'

'Who has it then?' I asked.

'P'raps it's you,' Crikky said – rather unkindly, I thought.

'I've got an ordinary cold,' I told them. 'I caught it from Jesus.'

The man in the manger laughed.

'Well, anyway,' Swallow said, 'this is our great opportunity to organise the Secret Society. Already we've told hundreds while you've been asleep.'

'Don't forget I had to have my alarum going off twice in the night,' I said. 'I'm dead, that's what I am.'

They kill me.

I looked at Jesus. He was sitting up, His hands round His knees. He'd been telling them stories or something. He looked very peaceful, and He smiled at me a lot.

'Brat saved my life at five-thirty with tea,' He said.

'When you others were all hogging it in your beds,' I reminded them, and put Bette Davis back in the manger with Him. 'What's the time?' I asked. Hell, I seem to be always asking the time. I'm going to take the money out of my money-box and *buy* a watch, I am really.

'Quarter to one,' Jeremy said. He's got such a big watch it takes up half his arm.

'Quarter to one! Migod, how time flies . . .'

Everyone started shuffling towards the door.

'Now don't forget your instructions,' Swallow warned them. 'And always remember, it's a secret from the grown-ups.'

They all nodded and beetled off.

Outside, this Charlie Staircase character was still smelling about.

'What's he after?' Poor Baby asked.

'He's on the track of something,' Swallow said. Then her hand flew to her mouth, like she'd thought of something.

'*Strange footmarks!*' she whispered. I nodded. Old Charlie Staircase was going to give the show away.

Poor Baby had hold of him in a second.

'We must shut him up in the nursery,' he said.

Naturally, we agreed.

After we'd done it we washed and tidied ourselves up for lunch and went down to the dining-room.

Actually we were keen to find out about the Added

Horror, and we reckoned if we sat about quietly, just stroking Bette Davis and not talking, we might get some news.

They were all in there when we opened the door. The whole lot.

They stopped talking and looked round at us in silence.

'Brat darling, I thought you were in bed with a cold,' Granny said.

'I was, all morning I was,' I answered, 'but I didn't want to give Cookie the trouble of taking up my tray, so I came down.'

'You're particularly thoughtful today, Brat,' Father said and laughed.

Well, I had to be.

'Don't you give me your cold,' Violet said, and moved farther away. 'I've only just lost one.'

'P'raps Brat found it,' Poor Baby said, and started on these peanuts.

'Why isn't anyone going to school?' I asked Father. 'Is there an epidemic?'

'Sort of,' he said and got out that old golden bottle.

Something's up, I thought.

'Is it the plague, then?' I asked.

'It certainly is a sort of plague,' Granny said, and old Cocky nearly nodded his head off.

A sort of plague!

We looked at each other trying not to show our delight. That would mean no school for months!

'It starts with a cold,' Violet said and laughed. Unkindly, I thought.

'Then you started it,' I told her.

'Brat,' said Father, 'that's rather cheeky.'

Granny sighed, and I knew she was thinking about wild animals.

'How long will it be before we can go back to school?' Swallow asked pleasantly.

'Oh, probably tomorrow or the next day,' Father said. 'It depends.'

'What does it depend on?' Poor Baby asked him, not quite so pleasantly.

'It's really nothing to do with you, darlings,' Granny poked in. 'I shouldn't ask any more questions if I were you.'

'But you're not us, Granny, and it *is* to do with us as it's our school which is caught up in this sort of plague,' I said very firmly.

'You can say that again,' Poor Baby added.

'Is it the sort of plague that makes people's noses drop off of them?' I asked again.

'Listen. I don't want to talk any more about it. So shut up!' Father handed a glass of this golden stuff to old Violet.

There wasn't anything more to say. We just sat in angry disconsolate lumps, waiting for lunch and wishing we hadn't come in early.

'What have you been doing, Merlin?' Granny asked him.

'Oh, playing,' he said, sort of off-handed.

'Playing what, darling?'

'Well – lots of things – mothers and fathers—'

He crammed his mouth with these peanuts.

'And you, Swallow dear? Mothers and fathers too?'

Golly, how she does hammer on.

Swallow shook her head and grinned.

'Oh no. I'm too old for that lousy game.'

This settled Granny for a while. We sat in silence. Then Violet started.

'What an extraordinary smell!' she said suddenly. 'What can it be?'

'Hope it's not the pheasant we're having for lunch,' old Cocky mumbled into his glass.

'It certainly isn't pheasant,' Violet said and began looking round the room.

Then they *all* started sniffing about. I don't know why they were making such a fuss.

I couldn't smell anything. But then I had this cold.

'P'raps it's Bette Davis,' I said helpfully. 'Maybe she's cut.'

After that all hell broke loose.

Granny let off one of these moaning 'Ohhhhs!' she does when she's upset, and old Cocky choked up his drink into the glass. As for Violet, she just let off this shriek, and before we knew where we were we were all outside the room, with Bette Davis, and the door was shut.

'Well, really!' I said. 'What a fuss – it *was* a possibility.'

'Father thought so too or he wouldn't have put B.D. out with us,' remarked Poor Baby dispassionately.

We messed about in the nursery after that. Poor Baby had a smoke, and I did a bit of crayoning.

'I wish we knew what all this plague talk is about,' Swallow said. 'I've a good mind to go and ask some grown-up.'

'Like Edward,' Poor Baby said, 'or maybe the Vicar. He'd be the best if you could catch him at an off moment.'

'He's always off,' I said. And so he is. Going like mad in the opposite direction.

'He's strictly honest,' Swallow said. 'He'd tell us the truth.'

Back in the dining-room for lunch, they seemed to have got over their upset and were quite conversational.

'Did you say hares and rabbits today?' Granny asked me.

I told her no.

'Did you, Granny?' Poor Baby asked.

'No, but I do like to say it,' she said.

Silly really.

All the time I kept finding Father looking round at us. He was watching out for this plague, and we knew it.

I started to itch a bit, all over my back, so I jerked my sweater around. You know, the way you do when you can't actually get at it.

'I think maybe I have purpura, after all,' I said.

'What's that?' old Cocky asked.

'Sometimes it's called the purples,' I said.

He started this laughing act of his again, and the others joined in. Father patted my back, and I was kind of pleased I'd made them laugh. But don't ask me why.

'Well, I s'pose you're glad you're away from school for a day or two,' he said.

I nodded.

'I am,' Poor Baby said. 'School isn't my best subject.'

'What is, then?' asked old Violet.

'Sleeping,' he said, and they laughed some more.

They slay me, these grown-ups, always yakking away at every darn thing you say.

I s'pose it was the bottle again.

After this we got on the subject of bats. This went on for an hour.

'And do you know, darlings,' Granny said, 'they hang upside-down in a dark place all winter and never eat a thing?'

We told her we did.

'But if the weather is warm they come out and fly about, you know.'

We told her we knew.

Then she started this story about her father having a huge long beard, and one day sitting out on some balcony in China – one of these bats got stuck in his beard. Pretty soon, after struggling with this bat to get it out of his beard, they had to get the nail scissors and cut the beard off.

She sat looking at us waiting for some remark. She got it from Poor Baby.

'Did he look any better?' he asked her.

And they went off into this laughing routine again.

'What are you all going to do this afternoon?' Father asked suddenly.

We all looked at each other and said absolutely nothing. Father went on:

'We could all go for a shoot.'

Nothing. Absolutely no word would come out of us.

'Or a movie. . . . How about a movie if we can find the right one?'

We knew there'd be a catch in it. It would have to be the *right* one – something corny.

'Thanks awfully, Dad, but actually we've got plans,' Swallow replied carefully.

'Plans? What plans?' he pressed on, helping himself to some of that disgusting cheese called Stilton.

'Well – actually, some of the kids are coming over and we were going to – well – play—'

'Fancy turning down a movie! Most unlike them, isn't it, Slim?' Granny remarked. She was quite astonished, she was really.

'Just as well, I've got plenty to do. But look here. I don't want you leaving the farm, understand?'

We nodded.

'You can mess around the fields nearby, but no one is to cross the road to the other farm.'

'Why not – as a matter of interest?' asked Poor Baby.

'Just because I say so,' he answered and got up from the table.

We went out to the goldfish pool, and stood in a clump so no one could hear what we had to say.

'There's something fishy,' Poor Baby said, staring at these goldfish.

'P'raps it's foot-and-mouth,' Swallow suggested.

We nodded.

I felt depressed, and said so.

'It's these fish, going round and round and having no purpose,' Poor Baby remarked. 'P'raps we should get out our fishing-rods and catch them.'

'What for?' I asked him idly. I didn't care really, but sometimes you just say things like that.

'To give them a change. We could put them in the bath for the afternoon,' he answered.

'Futile really,' I told him.

'Futile,' agreed Swallow. 'Anyway, what about *Him*?'

'P'raps we ought to change His hiding-place,' I suggested, but I knew that was futile too. Lousy, really.

'P'raps I'm getting this plague,' I said; 'I feel murderous.'

They both stared at me for a long time. Then Swallow shook her head.

'You look the same as ever,' was all she said.

'What about His lunch, then?' asked Poor Baby.

'It's not so easy to get Him anything decent.' Swallow was thinking hard. 'He must be sick of cake and milk, and I bet there's not a bone left of that pheasant.'

We all nodded gloomily. Actually I rather wished I was at school. There's always *something* to do there, sweets to eat or *something*.

'Here's old Elizabeth,' cried Poor Baby suddenly. And there she was. She had a sack she was humping along. Looked like a dead cat in it or something.

'What you got there?' I asked her.

'Tomatoes and things,' she answered straight away. 'And some old pie.'

'Good,' shouted Swallow, and ran towards her.

At the same moment round the corner came those two – Jeremy and Andrew. They had a bottle wrapped in newspaper. I always know bottles.

'What's in there?'

'Rum,' they said and undid it.

'Come *on*,' cried Swallow. 'Now He can have a decent meal, and if everyone brings something we'll have to have a storeroom.'

Jesus was pretty pleased to see the rum, and He fair fell on the tomatoes and ham. Elizabeth said it had been in the dustbin on account of their dog taking it into the garden, but Jesus didn't turn a hair.

We watched Him eat it. It looked better than the pheasant, and I started to feel hungry.

Crikky and Susan and Shirley and Pippa turned up pretty soon with bits of food, and some *Woman's Own* papers, but the only person who was interested in them was Bette Davis, and she used them at once.

'It *is* the plague,' Poor Baby said. 'Father as good as admitted it.'

'We couldn't get a word out of anyone,' the others said. 'But we notice everyone is suddenly rather nice to us.'

'That's because they know if we get this plague we'll all die,' I told them. 'And if people think you're going to die, they're always nice to you.'

'Not always,' Jesus said. His mouth was full of ham.

'I brought you some toothpaste,' Susan said. 'Do you like Euthymol or S.R. best?'

He thought about it for quite a long time before He answered:

'I don't want to be ungrateful,' He said, 'but I like Phillips best of all.'

'Rosanna and Jenny use Phillips,' Swallow said. 'We could get theirs.'

'S.R. will do nicely,' Jesus said, and He grinned at Susan as He took the toothbrush. The tube of S.R. was pretty mangled, but there was probably enough for a couple of brushings, I thought.

There were nine of us in here by now, plus Bette Davis and the calf. I thought if many more come we won't be able to move; we'll *have* to get ourselves into a bigger place.

'Look here,' I said to Swallow. 'This crowd is getting bigger every moment, and having this old calf in here is hellish dangerous; why don't we transfer to the top of the oast? There's only old yellow apples there; it won't be nearly such a strain.'

Everyone agreed, though I don't think Jesus looked too happy.

'We could move at night,' Poor Baby said.

I thought of my alarum and wished I'd never suggested it, I did really. I was dying for a good night's sleep.

'We daren't do it in the daylight,' Swallow said; then she turned to Him. 'We all think you should go up into the top of the oast, it's safer there. I mean Eric might get in here on account of this calf.'

'I think tonight, when you're all asleep, I should be on my way,' He said quietly, looking round at us.

'Where to?' asked Shirley. She's very practical.

'Oh – anywhere,' He replied; sort of sadly He said it. We rallied to His Cause.

'You're safer here with us than anywhere,' Jeremy said, and he was dead right, specially with the plague about.

'I've got it!' cried Jeremy. 'We can wrap a blanket all round Him, then if we see anyone we can say it's old Cocky playing with us!'

'S'posing it's old Cocky who asks the question?' I said quickly.

'Well – anyone you like to think of,' he said, kind of lame.

'Miss D.!' Swallow shrilled up. 'We can damn well say it's Miss D. come to play.'

'Correct,' said Poor Baby, and we all agreed.

Jesus wasn't keen to be Miss D. He wasn't keen at all to leave the manger, but we just went on with our plans and left Him with the rum and tomatoes. The ham was all finished.

First we got a lot of hay and stuff and made a sort of bed. We passed Eric and he only smiled, never said a word. Then we took His boots, wrapped up in the newspaper the rum came in, and hid them, and then Swallow had a genius thought and went and got some wellingtons belonging to Cookie. We stuffed these onto His feet. He could hardly get them on and they went all bent and looked madly funny. Then we got this blanket and wrapped it all over Him, head and all; and the procession started.

When we got to the outside door He sort of hung back.

'I say,' He said, 'I don't like it. I don't want to get you kids into trouble, and honestly I will if anyone sees me.'

'Don't you worry,' I told Him, 'you'll be as snug as a bug in this rug, and it's safe as houses there; no one ever goes except for apples, and the best have been eaten.'

Well, we got Him outside. He looked a bit funny with this blanket all over Him and these bent boots of Cookie's sticking out underneath. Susan was giggling like a fool, but we got Him out onto the drive. Then suddenly we saw Father and Violet and old Cocky coming towards us.

'What on earth?' said Father.

'It's a game,' I said in a relaxed sort of way. 'A game.'

'Who's in the rug?' he asked and old Cocky started to laugh.

'Miss D. It's Miss D. having a game,' I said, and everyone started pushing along the road to the oast.

'I say,' said Father, 'look here, you mustn't treat her like that. . . . Let her out at once.'

And he *started to grab at the blanket*!

'Unhand the lady! Poor Baby, I command you to let Miss D. go.'

Here he was pulling at the blanket, and we were all pushing him away and trying to laugh, but terrified, we were really. Suddenly from inside the blanket came a high-pitched lady's voice:

'I'm all right . . . really I'm rather enjoying myself.'

And the whole cortège of us shuffled quickly on towards the oast, while Father and the others laughed their heads off at the amusing picture of our schoolmistress being rushed along the road in a blanket.

By the time we had got to the top of the ladder and taken the blanket off Him we were all in a muck sweat.

'By golly!' said Poor Baby. 'We would have had egg all over our faces if he'd got the blanket off you!'

We all laughed pretty heartily, but the situation had been the grimmest we had yet encountered.

'Jolly smart of you, Sir, to make out you were Miss D.,' said Jeremy.

'Yes, Sir, it was, Sir.' Poor Baby must have suddenly realised he hadn't been too respectful up till now.

This small window is tiny really, and filthy, but we could still see them standing about and laughing and telling each other what a sport Miss D. turned out to be. Which, in point of fact, she's not.

'What'll we do when he asks Miss D. about it?' asked Pippa.

'What happens if he hangs about there and asks her in to tea!' Swallow moaned.

We watched for quite a long time, but after a while they moved off down the drive, and the coast seemed clear.

He seemed quite comfortable – more comfortable than He was before, to tell you the truth; I think He felt safer too, but on the whole He looked worried as hell while we were fixing this thing up to be more cosy.

Through the window we could see a couple more kids had arrived, a girl called Mary and her small brother Johnnie. They looked as if they had some sweets, so I went down the ladder and swanned about in front of them.

'Where is He?' asked Mary. 'Johnnie has something for Him. So have I.'

'Sweets?' I asked hopefully.

Mary nodded.

'Have you sworn in?' I asked her. She said they had, so I took them up.

'This is Mary,' I said to Jesus. 'She has some sweets.'

'Hullo, Mary,' He said, and she grinned at Him and held out a packet of liquorice allsorts. He took one and passed the bag round.

Johnnie had an old faded rose. Out of his mother's hat, I should think. He held it out to Jesus. He's pretty small, about five, and he'd lost his shoe on the way up.

'It's a flower,' he said shyly. 'It's not real, so it can't die.'

Jesus took it and stuck it in His button-hole. It looked a bit like a cabbage, but He didn't seem to care much.

'Thank you, chum; thank you very much,' He said.

'What a lot of friends I have. Without friends the world is a wilderness.'

I was doing my nut to understand what He meant, but I didn't ask Him.

'Talking of friends,' said Swallow, 'I think we ought to have a password. I mean, anyone can horn in here, friend or enemy.'

We all agreed.

'You could use my Society if you like,' I said. 'It's particularly good, if you know what I mean, because it's U.S.H., which means "Ush", which seems a particularly good and suitable word for the situation.'

'Ush . . . very good indeed,' said Swallow. 'Good show, Brat. And anyone who doesn't give the password isn't favourably disposed.'

U.S.H., of course, actually means Unrightful Slaughter of Horses, which is my favourite charity.

Jesus was laughing His head off by now. He certainly had a very good sense of humour.

'How sweet only to delight in lambs and laugh by
    streams,
To be a farmer's boy, and far from battle,'

He sang softly, looking at Poor Baby. It was some kind of poem, but none of us had heard it before. Probably by this man Longfeather.

'We ought to make hundreds of badges,' Poor Baby said. 'I'll get some paper and a pen.'

And he'd gone like the wind.

'We must swear, on pain of death, never to divulge,' Shirley said, and we all agreed it was the only thing.

The oast was pretty full of people by now, and I thought to myself it was a jolly good idea we had changed our locality, because if this plague scare was going on much longer there'd be hundreds of us in here, just hundreds, that's all. I posted myself at this small window where I could get a good view of the comings and goings. No one seemed much concerned with what we were doing up in the oast. Edward and the other men seemed to be gassing a bit to each other, but there didn't seem anything extraordinary about that. I saw Eric take this bucket of milk in to the calf, and thought what a merciful escape we'd had.

It was while I was watching Eric with this bucket that I suddenly saw Amos Nodge. I noticed him first because I could see the doves were a bit upset about something, then I realised he was running about among them kicking the hell out of them as if they were old autumn leaves. This got my goat, and before I knew what I was doing I was bashing away at the window with my fist.

'What are you *doing*?' cried Swallow, sharp as anything. 'You are an idiot.'

'It's Amos Nodge down there,' I said; 'he's kicking the hell out of the doves.'

'Well, we certainly don't want *him* to know we're here,' Shirley said. 'He's the sneak of all time.'

'I know,' I admitted, feeling a bit of a fool. 'All the same, I like those doves, and I don't like to see him going through them like a dose of salts, which is what he is.'

He couldn't have heard where the noise was coming from, as he was looking all around, but at least he'd stopped giving these birds murder.

'He didn't hear where it was coming from,' I assured

them. I was glad. He's a pretty good louse, Amos is; well, you can imagine the kind of background he must have with a name like that, anyway. I was beginning to breathe again when to my horror I saw Poor Baby tearing back with the pen and paper for these badges. He was coming down the hill so fast he didn't see this Amos. But Amos saw him. Poor Baby rushed into the bottom of the oast before he realised.

I could hear their voices at the bottom of the ladder. I warned all the others, and there was perfect silence in the top of the oast – like prayers at school before everyone gets up.

'Where you going with all that paper?' Amos was demanding.

'Nowhere,' Poor Baby answered.

'No one tears down a road to nowhere with their arms full of paper,' this Amos persisted. He's a right moron.

'Well, I can do what I like with my own paper in my own home, can't I?' asked Poor Baby. 'As a matter of fact I'm collecting a whole store of paper.'

'What for?' Amos had a deadly voice.

'Must I tell you everything?' Poor Baby asked again.

Amos didn't answer. I could see them through a crack in the boards. They were standing and just staring at each other.

Amos kicked a lump of dung into the air. He was trying to hit Poor Baby with it, but it didn't reach him. Poor Baby didn't budge an inch. Amos kicked a smaller bit. This got Poor Baby on the arm, but still he didn't budge.

'Stop kicking these cowpats about,' said Poor Baby.

'Why should I?' asked Amos.

'If you don't . . .' Poor Baby started.

'If I don't what?' asked the wretched boy.

'Nothing,' said Poor Baby. 'Just nothing; you aren't worth troubling about. I'm just going to put down my store of paper and leave you kicking the cowpats about if that's all you can think of to do.'

He put all the paper on this shelf near the door and turned round and walked out.

I could see Amos inspecting it pretty closely, but it *was* only paper, and pretty soon he gave it up and followed Poor Baby outside.

'Hey,' he called, 'where are the others?'

Poor Baby shrugged his shoulders and walked away up the hill.

In the top of the oast nobody moved. We could hear this Amos character coming back into the oast. We could hear him messing about with the paper. We could hear him fiddling about with the ladder.

It was a tricky moment.

I looked over to Swallow and made a huge sort of desperate face – you know, all teeth and eyes. She made for me not to move.

I craned over at the window and I could see Poor Baby standing about all miserable, with his eye on the door of the oast. I made for him to take Amos away. He was pretty cute; he didn't make any sign of having seen me, but he called out:

'Here, Amos!'

Amos didn't answer.

Poor Baby advanced to the bottom of the oast again.

'What the heck are you doing now?' he asked.

'Minding my own business,' was the reply.

'I'm going to have a swing, Amos. Like a swing?' Poor Baby began.

'No. I hate swings; they make me sick,' was the answer.

'They would,' said Poor Baby.

'You're just trying to get me away from here, that's what you're trying to do,' said Amos. 'Well, you won't succeed, so there.'

'I'm not trying to get you away. As far as I'm concerned you can wallow about in that muck all day if that's what you want, but let me tell you something. You'll catch tetanus, that's what you'll catch, and it's very catching.'

We all grinned. Good old Poor Baby.

'I've got to have a scratch first,' said this know-all.

'I'll pretty soon give you that,' said Poor Baby, and laughed.

'I'll tell my nanny,' Amos told him.

'I bet you will, you sneak!' said Poor Baby.

'I'm going up this ladder,' Amos went on.

'That's just stupid,' Poor Baby said. 'There's nothing up there, only rotten apples.'

'I like rotten apples. I eat rotten apples. I'm one of the few people in the world who love rotten apples,' Amos replied.

'Well, anyway, they're our rotten apples,' Poor Baby told him. 'Cookie would be furious. She makes marmalade with rotten apples. And if you go up there I'll take the ladder away and you'll never get down again.'

'Oh yes I will.'

'Oh no you won't.'

'I will.'

'You won't.'

'Will.'

'Won't.'

'Will.'

'Won't.'

This was getting monotonous.

'Well, I'm going,' said Poor Baby. His voice rose to a shout: *'But I warn you it's dangerous.'*

We knew he was warning *us*.

Poor Baby went out singing. I could see him wander off to the swing and sit on it.

Underneath us we could hear this Amos start to clamber up the ladder.

I got an idea. I sat down on the trap-door and made for the others to come and sit on it with me so he couldn't lift it. Pippa and the boys and Elizabeth all crept forward and sat on the trap-door.

He was at the top of the ladder by now. We could feel him heaving it up with his head.

Of course, it didn't move. We felt pretty safe.

'I know someone is up there,' said Amos, just under our bottoms. 'Tell you why: I can see Elizabeth's knickers.'

We didn't move. Didn't budge an inch.

'I can see Bette Davis' feet too,' the brute went on.

Still we didn't move.

Suddenly we saw Elizabeth's knickers starting to move. He was pulling at them.

She screwed up her face but she didn't say a word.

'I'll have your knickers off of you,' he shouted. Right under our bottoms he was.

Elizabeth's face was livid.

'Let me in, then,' he shouted.

No one answered or moved.

Jesus was doubled up with laughter, but mercifully no sound came.

'Come on, let me up. Why shouldn't I come up?' he bellowed.

No one answered a word.

'I'll go and tell.' He started snivelling. 'I'll go and tell!'

He was pulling madly at the girl's knickers by now and damn nearly did have them off of her.

There was a sudden tear, and half her knickers disappeared. Her eyes were enormous, but she stuck it. He was banging and yelling and carrying on alarming, when all of a sudden there was a crash and he'd fallen off the ladder into the manure.

God, how he yelled!

Jesus was laughing so hard He had to cram this straw all over His face.

Anyone would think Amos was being murdered.

Shriek after shriek.

We didn't move.

Through the window I could see Eric running, and Brian.

'What's up?' they called, and we could hear them splashing around underneath.

'Someone tried to kill me!' the little beast sobbed.

'Who did, *who* did?' Eric's voice was high as kites trying to drown this din.

But Amos just sobbed on noisily, like a fool.

'What did he do? Where did he get you?' Brian was asking. God knows why they were so hysterical.

But Amos just yelled. I know it was because he was all mucked up with these cow-pats, but Brian didn't seem to get it.

'Better get the boss right away,' Eric said, and tore out and down the drive like a lunatic.

We all sat – well, turned to stone, really we were.

I could see Brian messing about and trying to see where the little fool was hurt, but he was yelling so hard he couldn't speak.

'You're just scared, that's what you are,' said Brian consolingly, but this only made the louse yell louder.

Through the window we could see that Poor Baby had disappeared. Pretty wise of him, as there'd be questions if he stayed.

'Come on up to the house and get clean,' Brian was saying. 'Maybe Cookie'll give you a nice cuppa.'

'They tried to kill me!' bellowed the rat.

'Who, just tell me who?' Brian was shouting back. 'Was it a man? Was it a man?'

This Amos just went on yelling. And all the time not one of us moved.

By now Brian had got him outside of the oast and we could see him. He was totally immersed in muck. No wonder he yelled. I very likely would have done too. But then, I'm fastidious about things like that.

'There's only one thing,' said Swallow. 'We've got to get down before anyone comes up, it's the only hope.'

We didn't say a word. We just all got up and started trooping down this ladder.

At the bottom was a great hunk of Elizabeth's knickers.

When we got out we could see Eric haring back up the hill and Father with him.

Hell!

He was still yelling. Beats me how anyone could go on so long. Spoilt, I guess, and used to yelling.

'Some maniac,' I began.

'Where? Where?' Brian was behaving most oddly.

I didn't answer. I didn't understand a thing, honestly I didn't. Such a fuss about falling off a ladder. I mean, it wasn't as if cow-pattery is *hard* to fall on.

By now we were all standing about with egg on our faces, and Father had arrived, breathing heavily.

'What's the matter, Brian?' he asked. He seemed madly concerned.

'The boy is yelling that someone tried to kill him, and Brat has just said something about a maniac,' he drooled on.

Father turned to me.

'What maniac and where?' he demanded. His Adam's-apple was going up and down. I was so busy watching it I didn't answer.

'They all look pretty scared to me, sir,' Brian said.

Father got hold of Amos.

'Now tell me,' he said, 'where is this maniac that tried to kill you?'

'Up there,' Amos said and pointed at the oast.

We were riveted with horror.

'Come on, boys,' Dad shouted; 'let's get him.'

And he started towards the opening.

In a flash Swallow was in front of him, stopping him.

'Dad, Dad!' she cried. 'There's no one there at all. We've just come down, honestly. We were playing, and he tried to get up the ladder and like a fool he hung on to Elizabeth's knickers and they came apart and he fell off, that's all.'

Dad paused and looked at Amos.

'Is this true?' he asked.

Amos nodded.

Father was livid.

'Right,' he said, in that tone we all know so well. 'Straight up to your rooms, you two, and the rest of you go home.'

Without a word, they went.

'At once!' he yelled.

We fled.

His voice followed us.

'I'll deal with you two later.'

Four

We went up to our rooms.

Luckily for us we were all together, with the bathroom in between. We didn't say a word, Swallow and I. We were thinking pretty deeply; wondering, too, where Poor Baby had got to, and whether anyone would go up to the top of the oast after all.

From my window I could see the oast quite plainly. There was no one near it. It stood quietly in the afternoon sun the way I like to see it, with its wonky hat on the side and the green moss growing over the yellowed tiles. It seemed kind of crazy to think no one knew, except us, that Jesus was in there under that dotty-looking hat. And yet I was sort of confused about the whole thing, I was really. I imagine it was because I was still tired. I should like to have got straight into bed with Bette Davis and gone to sleep, but I didn't dare to, as I knew Father would be up in a moment.

I was feeling downright miserable. Sentimental really.

Sometimes I get these dreary feelings, lonely really, as if something weren't quite right. Once I told Cookie about them and she just said, 'It's growing pains.' I don't know what she meant; I just know I feel bloody sad, that's all.

I was feeling it now.

'I'm not happy,' said Swallow; 'about Amos, I mean. There's something dead mean about him, and we could be in for a lot of trouble.'

I agreed.

Father isn't often angry, but when he is like he was down by the oast we just feel awful – that's all, awful – because, you see, there isn't anyone else . . .

'I wonder what Poor Baby's up to,' Swallow said after a pause.

'He's no slouch,' I reminded her. 'He probably saw the whole thing from behind the rhododendron bushes; maybe he followed old Amos home and gave him a bashing.'

'Hope to Heaven no one went up to the oast,' she answered.

'What's going to be the end of all this, Swallow?' I asked.

'What do you mean?' she said. She was sharpening pencils to keep herself steady.

'Well . . . Jesus really . . . I mean, how long are we going to keep Him a secret, and why does He keep saying He has to move on? . . . and, anyway, wouldn't the grown-ups be pleased to find Him?'

Swallow shook her head.

'Something tells me they wouldn't treat Him right. Something tells me that,' she said quietly.

We couldn't go on with our talk on account of Poor Baby arrived suddenly. He had a load of paper and scissors and pens.

'Thought we'd get on with the badges,' he said and passed some paper over to us.

He'd cut out a round and printed U.S.H. in the middle with his Biro.

'What happened to Amos?' I asked while I was cutting out the paper.

'Eric took him home. My God, what a shindy!' said Poor Baby.

'Everyone was so het up about nothing,' said Swallow. 'Goodness, we've often pushed people off haystacks and things and no one has cared much.'

'He kept on saying someone was murdering him, silly clot,' Poor Baby replied. 'And no kidding, I'd have liked to do just that.'

'There's no one up in the oast to look after *Him*,' Swallow said, but Poor Baby waved his arms around.

'He's okay,' he said. 'No one went up after you'd gone. They just stood around whispering. Couldn't hear a word.'

'I think I'd like a cigarette,' I said suddenly; 'I'm all on edge.'

Poor Baby handed me his packet, but I'm not much good at rolling cigs, so I gave the whole idea up and got onto my bed and lay down.

'Hope I'm not in for the plague,' I said. 'I feel bloody awful.'

It was at this second that Father opened the door and came in.

He eyed us vaguely. He didn't seem as cross as we expected.

'Hullo, Dad,' said Poor Baby brightly.

'What are you doing with all that paper?' asked Father.

'Making badges for Brat's Society, you know, the "Unrightful Slaughter of Horses",' and he held up the badge for him to see.

Father sat on the end of my bed.

'You know, you are idiots; you might have hurt that twerp of a boy, pushing him off the ladder.'

'We didn't push him, Dad,' Swallow said hotly. 'We just didn't want him up there and pretended not to be there and he saw Elizabeth's knickers showing through the crack and held on and they broke and he fell off.'

'He yelled because of the manure,' I told him. 'Anyone would yell falling face down into cowpats. I woulda.'

'Why wouldn't you let him up?' Dad asked. 'There were lots of others there.'

'We just don't go for Amos Nodge,' I replied. 'Don't go for him at all.'

'It's not a very Christian attitude, is it?' Father asked and looked round at all of us.

We smelled a rat.

We didn't answer.

'I s'pose I made more of it than I usually would, because I was scared,' he went on. He picked up some of the paper as he was talking and started writing U.S.H. on the badges.

'Scared?' asked Poor Baby. 'Scared of what?'

'All that yelling blue murder,' said Father. 'You never know what kind of characters are around these days.'

'No, you don't, do you?' I said carefully.

'Have any of you seen any strangers about?' He looked round at us again. 'Strange men? Or just one strange man you don't know?'

He was looking at me because he was on my bed.

I shook my head firmly.

'No strangers at all,' I said. 'None of us have.'

'None of us,' agreed Swallow and Poor Baby together.

'That's all right, then. But if you do you must tell me at once. Understand?'

'Yes, Dad.' We all said it at once.

He got up off the bed.

'Why, Dad?' asked Swallow.

'Well . . .' He hesitated.

'Is it something to do with the plague?' asked Poor Baby.

Father nodded.

'It is, in a way.'

'You mean, some stranger has this plague?' I asked.

He nodded again.

'Well, all right, you can leave your rooms now, but remember, stick around the farm, and let me know if you see a stranger.'

Then he went.

Swallow followed him to the door to see he wasn't listening outside. Grown-ups do. Specially Violet.

'Corks!' said Poor Baby.

I knew what he was thinking.

'*He* couldn't have this plague,' I told him.

'He had a one-o-one temperature, didn't He?' asked Poor Baby.

'Know what I think?' I asked them. They said they didn't.

'I think we should tell Dad about Jesus.'

'I think we should ask Him first if He wants us to,' said Swallow.

We agreed.

It was teatime when we got downstairs, but no one was there only Granny, eating a hot bun.

'Enjoyed your holiday from school, darlings?' she asked.

'Sort of,' I said. 'I feel so darn tired, I do really. P'raps I *am* getting this plague. I've suggested it to a few people, but no one seems to give a damn.'

'Oh, darling, I do.' She seemed quite concerned. 'Have you got a temperature, I wonder?'

'She's just tired, she had a bad night,' Poor Baby told Granny.

'Well, have a bun,' Granny said, and I took the biggest.

We all chewed on in silence, thinking our own thoughts.

Granny seemed to be concerned with her own thoughts, too; she got up and started watering these hyacinths. She's forever pouring water onto plants all over the house, then they drip down and you have to rush and get her a rag or something before the carpet's messed up. Sometimes Bette Davis gets accused of these dribbles, which isn't fair as she's very responsible for her size, and always, but always, searches out these newspapers, and if she can't find one on the floor she'll select one that somebody is reading.

'I wish I knew how long we were going to be away from school,' Swallow said after a moment.

'Only until the scare is over,' Granny said.

'Scare?' I asked, hoping to catch her off guard.

'The police will say when you can go back,' Granny went on. She'd dropped some water on the table now and was getting anxious. I gave her my hankie from round my neck. She dabbed at the pool madly.

'The police?' asked Swallow curiously. 'What have the police to do with the plague?'

'Well, dear, it's really not exactly the plague as you know it. That was merely a play on words.'

What *was* she talking about? . . .

'I see,' said Swallow cautiously – not wanting to upset the apple-cart, as it were, though of course she hadn't the least idea what Granny was talking about either.

'The police have a finger in every pie, don't they?' added Poor Baby.

'It's their job to guard us all,' Granny replied, sort of proudly.

'Granny,' I said, sort of wheedling, 'what exactly have the police to do with it?'

'Only their job as protectors of the law,' she replied.

We were getting nowhere with this conversation.

'The world is full of very funny people these days,' she went on. She just loves to have the chance of talking with no one interrupting, and if you give her half a chance she'll really run on, so we were cute enough to say nothing, and just listen, maddening as it was watching her bumbling round this room wetting all these plants.

'When I was a little girl the world was a much safer place; people were kinder and nicer to each other. Things didn't go so fast. We used to go in carriages. It was a beautiful time.'

'Some carriages can go like hell,' Poor Baby reminded her. 'I've seen Harold going like crazy along the road by his house, and that old horse is just about the most dangerous animal alive.'

'I'm talking of well-bred carriages.' Granny was being a bit snobbish, I thought. 'Yes, the world has changed horribly,' she went on. 'All values seem to have gone; everywhere you look there are murderers and rock-and-roll, and strikes and rumours of wars.'

We're off, I thought. She'll never stop now, and bit by bit she'll go off the subject. I brought it back.

'But there are even more police, I s'pose,' I said hopefully.

'They're not always successful. They can't be; there aren't enough of them to cope with all these horrors. Goodness, in my young day I wouldn't have thought twice about walking down the lane at night. I wouldn't dare now.'

'Why not?' We shot the words at her.

'I'd be afraid someone would bounce out at me,' she said at once. 'And you children, every day you're in danger of some assault; it's terrible, terrible. I blame the television; I think it's a dreadful institution.'

'What's the television got to do with bouncers out at you?' Poor Baby asked her.

'Violence everywhere. It puts ideas into people's heads, and they get away with murder,' she replied.

'Actually, Granny, they don't,' I said. 'There's always goodies and baddies, and the goodies always win. That's what's so boring,' I said, and it is.

'And *no* one has any religion,' she went on.

Goodo, we were on the right track now.

'We have,' I said. 'I mean, we believe in Jesus coming again to put everything right. Do you, Granny?'

'I certainly do. It's the only hope. I'm afraid if He came again now He'd have a lot of trouble making people believe in Him.'

'Really?' asked Swallow. 'I wouldn't have any trouble nor would Brat and Poor Baby.'

'Children are so trustful,' she said. 'That's the trouble.'

She didn't make sense, she didn't really.

'But there it is, we have all got to become like little children before He comes again.'

If all the grown-ups became like children it would be a pretty smashing world, I thought.

'If someone came up to you and told you He was Jesus, would you believe Him?' Poor Baby asked.

'Depends,' answered Granny. 'Lots of people have said they *were*, but they were lunatics.'

It seemed to me she was going to be just as stubborn as all the people she was condemning.

Grown-ups kill me. I don't think they know what they're talking about most of the time.

'Granny,' said Swallow. 'If we told you a secret, would you *swear* not to tell a soul?'

Dangerous, I thought, dangerous as hell. I don't s'pose she's kept a secret ever.

I made a ghastly face behind her back at Swallow.

Granny turned round and looked at us. She looked interested, almost cunning. I didn't like the look of it at all. Neither did Swallow, I could see that.

'Of *course*, darling. You can tell me anything you like and I'll never breathe a word.'

She waited.

'What is it, darling?'

'Nothing,' said Swallow. 'Just a new society we were building up we thought you'd like to join; we'll tell you about it later.'

Granny looked hellish disappointed.

Luckily for us some of the kids appeared at the window and made signs for us to come on outside.

We went.

It was getting a bit dark, but we could see there

were a lot of them. Swallow said to come on up to the nursery. It's private there and we can talk without being disturbed.

'Something the matter?' she asked.

I noticed they were all wearing their badges. You know, U.S.H. There must have been about twelve of them in there, all looking mysterious.

'Amos told his nanny,' said Jeremy.

'Who cares?' Poor Baby replied.

'I haven't finished yet,' Jeremy went on. 'His nanny told our cook that the police were looking for a *man*, and that's why your Father was in such a flap.'

'What man?' we asked.

'She said the police say he's an escaped convict and that's why there's no school,' Andrew whispered.

'Jesus *and* an escaped convict in two days,' said Poor Baby.

'The trouble is,' said Shirley, 'that these policemen may catch *Him* and say He's a convict!'

'How can they? I mean, they know what this convict looks like, don't they?' Swallow asked.

'But you know how idiotic grown-ups are, they just won't believe it's *Him*; they'll arrest Him and put Him into jail!' Shirley sounded desperate.

'He could get out of anywhere; He could perform a miracle, that's what I say,' said Pippa.

'He didn't last time,' Elizabeth reminded us. 'He couldn't get out of that last jam; it might happen again.'

This was a thought.

'P'raps He isn't Jesus,' said Crikky. 'P'raps He is a convict.'

Swallow gave him a look.

We stood around and thought.

'We could ask Him straight out if He's a convict, couldn't we?' Jenny suggested.

'He could still be Jesus,' said Elizabeth. 'It says in the Bible about not knowing who ye may be encounterin'.'

That was a thought. True, too.

'If He was a baddie He'd be caught, anyway,' Poor Baby said. 'They always are in the end; it's a sort of – well – rule. Baddies never get away with it. Goodies always win; even though it's boring, it's a sort of rule of life. Don't ask me why.'

Personally, I've always been on the side of these baddies. They have a pretty raw deal, I always think. I've always agreed with myself that I wouldn't give them away if I had a chance. I mean, I'm always pretty sorry for the people who seem to be losing, unless they're downright lousy.

'What'll we do, then?' asked Susan again.

'Nothing,' said Swallow. 'Just nothing, that's all. If He's who we know He is, and He doesn't want to be caught again, there'll be something, angels or something, that will save Him. In the meantime it's up to us to help.'

Good show, I thought. It makes sense.

'Come on, then,' she said. 'Let's go and see Him; let's go and talk to Him about it.'

We crept out so no one would see us, and somehow got back into the top of the oast.

He was still there. He didn't look a baddie at all. He smiled at us all, just as He always had done.

He had a nice face. Odd thing though, if I met Him again now I don't believe I'd remember Him. I never really got His face stuck in my mind, nor did the others, they said afterwards.

He had nice eyes. Blue.

'Something the matter, kids?' He asked, still smiling.

'Correct,' said Poor Baby.

'We're in trouble,' said Swallow. 'Not about Amos, though there's still a possibility of that; it's this story we hear around.'

'Oh?' He said.

'Yes,' she said. 'Jeremy heard his cook say they were looking for a convict.'

'Ah!' was all He said, and scratched His neck. S'pose the straw was tickling Him.

'Are you Him, or are you who they're looking for?' asked Crikky.

'How do you know I'm not both?' He asked quietly.

This was a poser.

No one answered.

'Could you be both?' asked Crikky; his eyes were absolutely bulging.

'Course,' Elizabeth said loudly. 'Well, you know, sent as a convict instead of a fishmonger – and, goodness, that's nothing! Some convicts are quite nice; our gardener knows hundreds.'

The man looked round at all of us.

'I never said who I was, did I? I never told you what my name was or anything, did I?'

'Well, actually,' said Swallow, 'you did.'

'Oh? When?' He asked.

'It was when you first got here, the day you came into that other place. "Who are you?" Elizabeth said, and you just looked round, and said "*Jeezus*" – just like that, you did really; didn't He, Elizabeth?'

Elizabeth nodded her head like mad.

'And we believed,' she said sort of proudly.

The man didn't move or say anything. Actually He looked a bit miserable. There's something pretty nice about Him, I thought, every sign of being a goodie. He looked up at Poor Baby, who was standing beside Him and sucking this straw.

'What you think about it all, Chum?' He asked. I got the idea He rather liked Poor Baby.

'I'm just racking my brain, that's all,' Poor Baby answered. 'Just racking the hell out of my brain.'

We stood about. It's all this television and things, I was thinking to myself, all this talk of goodies and baddies; I was beginning to agree with Granny, I was really.

'It's a terrible institution,' I said.

The man laughed. I don't think He knew what I was talking about.

I could see everyone was thinking furiously. It was like school when some corny question had been asked and no one knew the answer. I looked at Poor Baby; he was still sucking the heck out of this straw, and scratching a lump of plaster off the wall with his finger.

The Man said nothing. He just kept on looking round at all of us.

The silence was awful. Then Poor Baby spoke.

'You know what I hate? I hate sneaks,' he said. 'Everyone is always telling us not to be sneaks, and that's just what that Amos Nodge turned out to be. A sneak.'

'There always has to be a sneak in the story,' Elizabeth told us. 'Last time he was called Judas.'

'I like the name Judas better than Amos,' said Pippa.

It was getting pretty dark in here by now. No one had lit this hurricane lamp, and I could hardly see anyone's face.

Right by me Bette Davis had spent a penny on a magazine – right on the words 'The truth about golf balls'.

Elizabeth started to cry. She put her head on His knee and just cried.

I hate crying. It puts me on edge.

He patted her head.

'I don't care who you are or what you are,' she said. 'I just hate things being caught – just hate it, that's all.'

Well, we all agreed with that.

'I mean, where are these angels?' she asked, looking up into His face.

She believes madly in angels on account of she's actually seen them.

'I reckon this room is full of them,' He said quietly, looking round at us. This cheered her up a lot, and she wiped her eyes with the back of her hand.

I was quite close to Him, and I could see how ragged He seemed to look. I'm a sucker for ragged things, I am really. These smart shiny things never seem to get me the way the ragged ones do. Old toys and things, and sweaters. One's sorry for these ragged old things. They look squashed, like nobody cares for them any more, and when they were new and shiny everyone was mad about them. Left about, that's what they were. That's what He looked. Just left about.

'Look here,' He said suddenly, 'I think I'll be on my

way. You just all stay here and go on talking, and I'll slip down that ladder and clear off.'

'That would be awful,' said Jeremy, 'just awful somehow.'

'S'pose you think that would be running away,' the Man said slowly.

'Actually I do, sir,' said Mark. 'Otherwise, why do you?'

'Actually, because I don't want to get any of you into trouble, or embarrass you.' He looked round. 'D'you understand what I mean?'

We didn't, really. I mean, *we* aren't ever embarrassed, not at all except at things like seeing Granny's camiknickers hanging down, and that's different; it's just because of the indecision of knowing whether to point it out to her or not.

'You're a great bunch,' He said. 'I'll never forget you. You've taught me a great lesson.'

I happened to be looking out of this window. I happened to see a couple of figures walking up the road.

I made a signal to Swallow and she came over.

'Who're these?' I asked her.

Actually I knew.

'These are policemen,' she said. Very quietly she said it, and looked round at the others.

We all looked at Him.

Swallow got excited.

'It's History repeating,' she said, rather grandly, I thought.

'It's the soldiers coming to take You away again. But this time Your disciples are *not* sleeping.'

A terrible look came over His face. He really looked as

if something had hurt Him frightfully. You know, like when you get your thumb caught in the door. Like you're going to cry.

'That's settled it,' He said. 'I must go.'

'They've gone past,' Poor Baby told Him. 'Gone up to the house. They're after this convict they're looking for.'

'Are you a convict, sir?' asked Mary.

He smiled at her.

'What's a convict mean to you, Mary?'

'I don't know,' she said; 'I never saw one.'

She's only eight, so she couldn't have. Silly thing.

'It's someone what's done something wrong,' said Crikky.

'Like killing someone,' Jeremy added.

'Like stealing the sheriff's money, and holding up the stage-coach,' said Susan.

'Like the one in that film who booed out at people from behind graves,' said Poor Baby. 'I adored him. I cried when he died.'

'I still don't know what a convict is,' said Mary. Really slow she is.

'A convict is a man who is proved guilty of a crime by the law,' He told her. 'Sentenced to punishment. Prison, maybe death.'

'Last time You were *proved* guilty,' said Elizabeth. 'Sentenced too, and crucified, wasn't You? And then all those years afterwards they found out they were wrong!'

She turned to me and pinched the hell out of my bare arm because I was the nearest.

'Ouch!' I said.

Swallow got excited again.

'You see? It's the same old thing, the same old men, only now they're dressed as policemen! They're just going to make the same crashing silly mistake, and it's up to us to stop it on account of we *know*! Let's face it: they *are* grown-ups, you know.'

The Man put His head in His hands like He was thinking hard, and sighed madly hard.

'I don't know what to say to you people,' He said after a moment. 'Really, I don't know what to say.'

'Why?' I asked Him.

'I'll just say this, Brat, and don't you forget it ever. We're all on our own, see? Every man jack of us is on our own. We've got our own lives to live and no one can live it for us. Sort of hermit crabs we are.'

'They live in *drains*!' said Poor Baby.

He knows, he collected some at Rye.

'Well, maybe some of us live in big old drains at that,' said the Man, but He was laughing. I could see His teeth. 'I just meant we're all responsible for ourselves. Me for myself – you for yourselves. No one can really save anyone else. Know that?'

I was as confused as hell, I knew that. I bet the others were too. Then I remembered what happened to me when I was very young.

I was alone in these woods at the back of the farm. *Huge* great trees were all around me with this jade green moss on them. I could hear the herons calling each other down on the marsh. Lonely sad old croaky noises. Suddenly there wasn't anyone in the world but me, and I ran. I was quite out of breath when I saw old Edward by the silage heap.

'What's up with you?' he asked.

'I was suddenly afraid,' I told him.

'Afraid of what?' he asked.

'I didn't think there was anyone in the whole wide world but me,' I replied. 'I was afraid of being turned into a heron.'

'That's right,' he said, bashing at this silage. 'You'd have your own pair of wings, wouldn't you? Everyone has their own pair of wings.'

I never forgot that. Sometimes when I'm in one of my moods it cheers me up.

Of course you can't *see* them.

'I know what you mean,' I told Him. 'I know just what you mean.'

He looked at me and grinned.

'You do? Then you explain to the others.'

'It's nothing complicated,' I told them. 'It's like being birds, that's all. You can't see them of course, but it's like having wings, and no one can do the flying for you. You got to do it yourself.'

'Well done, kid,' He said. 'That's just it.'

'So what?' asked Crikky.

'So I have to look out for myself,' He said, 'in the end.'

'You didn't do very well last time,' Susan reminded Him.

'That was how it was meant to be,' Elizabeth told her. 'Maybe there's another plan this time too. Is there?' she asked Him.

He nodded.

'Does it turn out all right for you this time?' asked Poor Baby.

'It depends,' He said slowly.

'What does it depend on?' I asked.

'Same as last time – how I behave,' He replied.

'Tell you one thing,' I said. 'We know how *we're* going to behave, and we're not going to breathe one word about you. That's what U.S.H. is for.'

They all agreed.

It was getting to be pretty dark, but I could see the last bit of light shining on our badges. Looked pretty good to me.

'What's it mean? U.S.H.?' He asked.

'Well, actually,' I said, 'it means a Society for the Unrightful Slaughter of Horses, but it's useful because in this case it means "Ush".'

'That means keep your mouth shut,' said Swallow. 'It means we're all sworn to secrecy not to give you away.'

'All this for a stranger,' He sort of sighed again.

'*What* a stranger!' said Poor Baby in a holy sort of way.

'You *really* believe, don't you?' He asked. '*Really* believe I'm . . . well, who you think I am?'

'You bet,' said Jeremy.

'Would anything make you change your minds?' He asked.

'Like what?' I demanded.

'Well, supposing I told you I was a wicked convict who had done something bad . . . what would you think then?'

'We'd know that there was a good reason for You to say it,' replied Elizabeth. 'But it wouldn't make us change our minds. We'd know the truth, wouldn't we?'

She appealed to us all round the oast.

'Golly, yes, we'd know the truth all right,' said Rosanna.

He didn't answer. He was looking out of the window to where the night was coming.

'I should like to have lived here as a child,' He said sort of pensively. 'In this farm among the orchards and fields. Life might have been a whole lot different.'

'There would have been some rabbits then,' said Poor Baby. 'But we've had this mixamatosis.'

He laughed and got up out of the straw.

'Lost me old boots,' He said to Himself.

Poor Baby struck this match and we had a good look round. That's when we suddenly saw His feet.

Nice feet. Not bunionish like some grown-ups and all gnarled and beastly. But – well, straight really. Clean too, and in the middle of each of them were these holes.

'If nothing else had made us believe, the holes in your feet would have, sir,' said Mark.

'How did you get them holes?' asked Susan.

I turned on her, I did really.

'Honestly, Susan!' I said. 'Don't be so *idiotic*! Pull your finger out!'

'Well, I was only asking,' she muttered.

'Quite right too,' He said. 'What would you say if I told you I'd shot myself right through them, with a rifle, in nineteen forty-two?'

That killed us. We laughed our heads off, we did really. Susan looked a bit of a twerp. This made her give my pony tail a wrench, and it hurt like hell on account of these tight hairs.

He'd found His boots and socks by now and sat on the straw again, pulling them on.

'I hope this doesn't mean you're thinking of pushing on?' I said. I'd heard Father say it to a visitor once.

'There's a time for everything, Brat, and the time of my departure is mighty close at hand.'

'What a swizz!' I said.

'What about the police and all that?' asked Crikky.

'I'm not really worried about a few chaps in uniform,' He said. He pulled the shoelace so hard it broke.

'Blast!' He said.

'You can have my hair ribbon,' I told Him. 'It's pretty ropey but it'll do.'

He seemed quite pleased with it, and – well, really I must say I felt madly proud to think of my hair ribbon doing up Jesus' shoe.

'I hate like hell to think of you going out there,' said Swallow, 'I do really. I mean, I don't think those policemen looked all that nice.'

'About as nice as rattlesnakes,' He said, and we all laughed, but we felt sad. We weren't going to like His going away. We'd got used to Him, and somehow now there wasn't any more purpose. I told Him so.

'Thank you, Brat,' He said softly. 'Anyone got a handkerchief or a bit of rag to spare?'

'Not to cry on?' I asked nervously.

'No, just to tie round the old neck,' He said. 'It's a bit nippy out there.'

'Specially after a one-o-one temperature,' said Swallow, and she took her cardigan off and tied it round His neck.

'Oh no, Swallow honey,' He said, 'I don't want to take your jersey.'

'I'd be proud,' she said. She was nearly in tears, she was really.

'Here,' said Poor Baby. 'You've got Brat's ribbon on

your boot and Swallow's cardigan on your neck, what can I give you?'

'You've all given me plenty,' He said and stooped down and picked up Bette Davis and kissed her.

'Goodbye, old sweat,' He said to her. 'You kept me nice and warm, you did,' and then He put her back onto the *Saturday Evening Post*.

He seemed to be ready to go after that and stood there looking at us all.

It was at this point that Poor Baby gave Him his knife. It's a cowboy knife on a huge long string and he's pretty proud of it.

'Take this,' he said. 'You might need it to cut someone's throat with.'

The Man laughed like a drain, He did really.

'I give up,' He said, 'I just give up. You kill me, the lot of you.'

But He took the knife.

I s'pose He didn't want to hurt Poor Baby's feelings.

'Don't go,' begged Swallow. 'Please don't go, not yet. Wait and see. They'll catch the right convict, then they'll leave you alone.'

'The right one?' He asked. 'I thought we'd all agreed it was to be me.'

'Goodness, no! We all know who *you* are,' said Elizabeth. 'Nothing, just nothing will make us think different, so you don't have to worry about us. We believe. It's these grown-ups you've got to sort out.'

'I see,' He said thoughtfully, then He sat down again.

'Look here, sir, you're safer up here than anywhere,' said Mark.

117

He looked up at Mark; he's pretty tall and his head was in the dark.

'It's all written, you know, boy,' He said.

'I think it's just ghastly,' said Poor Baby, 'that you have to keep on coming back and getting got. It doesn't make sense, it doesn't really.'

'Isn't there any end to it?' I asked Him.

'There isn't any end to anything,' He replied, 'but as long as you don't mind too much I s'pose it doesn't matter either.'

'You're just *used* to it, aren't you?' asked Crikky. 'Mum says you get used to anything after a while.'

'That's the way to look at it, Chum,' He said.

'When we're grown-ups,' I said sort of drooly, 'that's when it'll be different, you'll see. You'll have a different reception when we're grown-ups.'

'Will I?' He asked me, kind of wearily, and stroked my face.

'When we run the world there'll be a purpose,' said Swallow.

'No schools,' said Susan.

'Or policemen,' said Crikky.

'Or caning,' said Andrew.

'Or notices which say "Keep off the grass",' said Pippa.

'Or atom bombs,' said Mark.

'Or death or dustbins,' I said.

He was still stroking my cheek.

'No death or dustbins, eh, Brat? What a great world you'll all make it. I'd like to be here then. P'raps there won't be any more wars or passports, misery, or starvation, or fear, or shame. I shall look forward to your world. Let's see, that will be in about – fifteen years' time.'

'Golly, that's *years*,' said Poor Baby. 'I'll be quite old.'

'You could be dead,' said Susan. 'Our Chip died – dead on fifteen years.'

He was a dog, I'd like you to know, so of course he was really a hundred and five.

'If I had a wish,' said Swallow, 'I'd wish you could suddenly be caught up, right in front of us, then we'd know you were going to be all right.'

'If I had a wish,' said Poor Baby, 'I'd wish Brat's bosoms would grow, so I could have my own bathroom.'

'If I had a wish,' the Man said, 'I'd ask for a cig, just a couple of puffs.'

'Good Lord, why didn't you say so before?' Poor Baby answered Him. 'I've got half a tin of papers and baccy.' He struggled in his jeans and brought out this half-mangled tin, which he gave to Jesus. He looked delighted, pleased as punch.

Poor Baby watched Him rolling one. Then the Man offered him the tin back.

'Keep it,' said Poor Baby. 'I'm giving it up for Lent, anyway.'

He seemed to be enjoying His puffs, but on the whole you could say He looked pretty fed-up. I got the feeling He wanted to say something, or maybe He wasn't sure whether He wanted to go or stay.

Nobody said much for a time. We just sat there in this almost dark, sniffing the smoke from His cig.

I don't know what the others were thinking, but I felt like I was seeing a train off. Mind you, I've never seen anyone off who I wasn't quite glad to say goodbye to. It's this train, I think, that seems to get you; it just keeps stopping and going, and people get on and off; I mean, no one, but no one, ever *looks* at this engine. Don't ask me why, because I can't explain, but sitting in here with Him, sort of waiting, was to do with trains.

'You know what I think?' He said suddenly.

We said we didn't.

'I think you should all vamoose.'

We must have looked a bit blank, our French is pretty bad.

'I think you should all disperse, go now.'

'Do you want to be alone to pray?' Elizabeth asked.

He looked madly solemn.

'Yes,' He said.

'I absolutely refuse to be caught sleeping,' Swallow told Him.

'Me too,' said some of the others.

'After you've said your prayers,' I asked Him, 'will you just wait to get took, or will you make a dash for it?'

'What do you suggest?' He asked.

'A dash every time,' I replied. 'Or is it against the rules?'

'P'raps I'll have to let myself get took,' He said, sort of sadly.

'On it goes,' said Poor Baby bitterly, 'the same old story all over again; it gets me down, it does really.'

'It doesn't *have* to happen that way,' said Mark suddenly. 'We could change it if we want to, because we *know*. The others, last time, weren't in on it, as you might say.'

'Correct,' said Poor Baby.

'Last time you never had a chance,' Swallow said

excitedly. 'This time we could hold them up, by golly, hold the lousy soldiers up, and give you a chance.'

'They'll get Him in the end,' said Susan. 'They always get everyone in the end.'

'You're right, kid,' He said. We could see the end of His cig burning, like a great red eye.

Just at that moment we heard this bugle of Father's.

'Corks!' said Poor Baby. 'That's a summons, that is.'

'It can't be bath-time,' Swallow said, and fiddled about with this clock of hers that's luminous. 'It's only quarter past six.'

'We better go and see what it's all about,' I said. 'What will you other characters do?'

'We'll go and round everyone up,' said Jeremy. 'Give them orders in case of disaster.'

'Good show,' said Poor Baby, and started for the ladder.

'I may not see you again,' said the Man and put His hand out.

We all stopped.

'Why not?' I asked. 'We'll be right back.'

'All the same, better say goodbye to be on the safe side,' He went on.

'Are you going to leave us, after all?' Swallow asked.

'Somehow—' He began and then stopped. We waited. 'Well – somehow, I don't think I'll ever leave you.'

'Oh, don't go,' Poor Baby begged. 'After all the trouble we've had with the badges.'

'They could go on being for the Unrightful Slaughter of Horses,' He said softly.

'That's what the grown-ups will think,' said Crikky, 'but we'll know different.'

'What words would it mean if it wasn't the horses' one?' asked Andrew.

'Unintentionally 'Scovered Him,' said Elizabeth.

'United States of Hamerica,' suggested Susan.

'You can do better than that!' I said loftily.

'Well, you try,' she snapped back.

'We'll keep them, anyway,' I told Him. 'And next time you come you'll know us by our badges, won't you?'

'I'll have lost mine,' said Poor Baby. 'Can't help it, but I lose everything.'

'You could put it in your cashbox,' said Swallow.

We could hear this bugle blaring.

He shook hands with us one by one as we went down the ladder. I stuck Bette Davis in my pocket. She was livid.

At the bottom we stopped and looked up. It seemed ghastly to think we might not see Him again. He was awfully nice. He was, really.

Outside the oast we all parted.

'You go and see what's up,' said Jeremy. 'Leave the rest to us, Mark and me and Andrew. We've got bicycles.'

They all hared away into the darkness.

It was just as we were getting to the rhododendron bush that we suddenly saw him. Amos Nodge!

'He's been listening!' I gasped.

'Judas!' shrieked Poor Baby and flung a lump of cowpat at him.

The little beast ran for his life, but we knew now, everything was desperate. But desperate.

In the sitting-room were these two corny-looking policemen, without their hats on. They grinned at us and made some lousy remark about cats' eyes in the dark or something pretty silly.

Father was there too. They all had glasses in their hands; and one had his glasses on his nose, at the end, looking at us over the top.

'Sergeant Porkers wants to ask you kids a few questions,' he said.

Porkers, I thought. Hope you aren't like your name sounds, rooting about all over the joint.

'Yes?' said Swallow, very confident.

'We wanted to ask you if you'd seen any strange men about,' said this Porker.

'No,' we said, 'only you two.'

They smiled grimly.

'Are you *sure*?' he went on.

The other one had a notebook and a pencil all poised ready.

'No one at all,' we said like a chorus of boys in church.

'It's my duty to warn you that there is a dangerous convict at a loose end,' he said, very serious. 'More than a convict – he's mentally unbalanced, and if he came across kids in a dark lane it might be the worse for them,' he added.

'Really? What would he do?' I asked.

'He might do anything. He might try to—'

Father cut in here:

'Serg. I don't think we want to frighten!'

'No, sir, of course not, but I do think these kids should have a good idea of their danger, you know.'

'He might try to what?' I asked. 'Strangle us? Dig a knife in us?'

He grinned in a pretty corny way.

'Well, seeing as you've put it in your own words, young lady—'

'You mean he's a murderer at large? A murderer of kids?'

'Now don't be scared—' he said.

'*I'm* not scared, not one bit,' I assured him. 'I'd like to see a murderer at large. I've only seen one on the television.'

'Hope to God you never do,' said Father fervently, like he was saying the Lord's Prayer.

'We know he's somewhere round here. We've traced him to within a few miles.'

'Is there a reward?' asked Poor Baby.

'Mercenary little brute,' said Father and laughed.

'I was thinking of Amos Nodge,' said Poor Baby under his breath.

'What does he look like?' asked Swallow.

'Big man. Black hair, dark eyes.'

'Any . . . any . . . special marks about him?' asked Swallow. I could see she was feeling a bit sick.

So was I.

'Nothing that comes to mind at the moment,' said this Porkers. 'But *anyone* you see, *anyone* . . . you must report it at once.'

'What did he do?' asked Swallow, sitting down suddenly.

'He killed a warder, if you want to know, with a hammer.'

'I s'pose that was when he was getting out,' said Poor Baby; 'the fool probably got in his way. I mean, what was he a convict for?'

'He ran over a woman . . . he was house-breaking . . .

he didn't stop . . . he was in for manslaughter, if you know what that is,' said Porkers. I don't think he liked Poor Baby much.

'Well . . . we haven't seen him, that's that,' I said. 'Now I think if you'll excuse me I'm going to my room to be sick a little.'

I marched out, and the others followed me.

I could hear this Porker and his friend laughing.

Father, I'm glad to say, was *not* laughing.

We went to my room. It's near the bathroom, and I had to sit on the can.

The others stood around me.

'Are you really going to be sick?' asked Swallow.

She has an absolute *horror* of sick.

'Damn nearly,' I said and gurked loudly.

'Here, give her the Alka-Seltzer,' said Poor Baby. 'That's her standby.'

He poured it out and gave it to me.

Swallow was looking away, in case.

'Well, there you are,' I said. 'If they catch Him they'll say He's the convict who ran over this corny dame who got in the way, not Jesus, I'd like to tell you!'

'I give up,' said Poor Baby. 'I'm more confused than I've ever been in my whole life. Why doesn't He admit it to the grown-ups and those two Porkers?'

'Hear, hear,' I said and meant it.

'That's how it's all Planned,' said Swallow. She was back now she didn't think I was going to be sick. 'It'll go on being this way till the grown-ups believe in something and have this Purpose.'

'There's that Nodge, he'll be up to a bit of no good with that Nanny of his,' Poor Baby said.

'When they've gone we'll go back and tell Him to take a chance and scram,' said Swallow. 'He likes us.'

'Is anyone beginning to doubt?' asked Poor Baby, sort of sly.

'I'm just confused. I really *am* a mixed-up kid,' said Swallow.

'I'm not,' I said. 'This old Alka-Seltzer's put me back on my feet. If it's the last thing I ever do I'm going to help Him get away.'

The others nodded.

'It's not as if we even knew this warder,' said Poor Baby.

'*Or* the dame he runned over,' I said, '*or* the people whose house he broke into. Damn it, they might have been some Nodges of this world. We've got to take Him as we see Him and know Him, and that's pretty good.'

'There's still a chance, anyway,' said Poor Baby. 'No one said anything about His feet.'

'Probably never saw Him with His boots off,' I said.

'Let's have a cigarette,' said Poor Baby. 'After that I'll give it up for Lent.'

He lit up, and opened the lavatory window, blowing the smoke out.

Suddenly he held up his hand, a signal for silence.

Underneath we heard a voice.

It came from the kitchen.

It was Amos Nodge's nanny!

We craned our necks.

'Little Amos swears there was a man up there, swears it. He could hear his voice, and it was a strange voice, talking to all those kids. That's why they didn't have him up there. Deceitful things.'

126

'Don't you talk about my kids like that, Gladys,' said Cookie.

Good old Cookie.

'Amos knows what's good and bad,' she went on.

She could say that again.

'Well,' said Cookie, 'if what you say is true, I'll have to tell the Master, but I think I'll ask the kids first.'

'Waste of time; they wouldn't tell the truth. I've always said they were wild as coots. Charles Addams kids, real Charles Addams, the three of them.'

Who's he when he's at home?

'Not a moment to lose,' said Swallow. 'One of us must go and warn the others. Better be me, as I'm the oldest.'

'I'm the fastest,' said Poor Baby. 'Don't forget my name!'

'All right, you go,' said Swallow. 'Give me a sip of your Alka-Seltzer to pull me round.'

'Have it all,' I said. 'I need another couple, I do really.'

Underneath, the talking had stopped.

Had she gone?

Was there still time to ambush her and put a sack over her head?

I asked Swallow.

'Probably shriek like a stuck pig,' she replied. 'Go down and engage her in conversation, compliment her on her hat or something.'

This was a joke of our Uncle Larry's. He's the hell of a guy, but always, literally *always*, in America.

I went down. With my Alka-Seltzer.

'Hullo,' I said to her and grinned.

She stared at me. She hates my guts.

'Have an Alka-Seltzer,' I said. 'Good for acid.'

'Who says I have acid?' she answered back.

'I can see you have,' I said. 'Your face is yellow, that's uric acid. Shouldn't be surprised if you aren't uric all over. This'll do the job,' I said.

Far from complimenting her on her hat, I was insulting her, and I knew it.

'Who is Charles Addams?' I asked.

'He's a very clever man. He's a drawer.'

'How can he be a man if he's a drawer?' I asked. 'Is it a riddle or something?'

'Cheeky, that's what you are,' she said and went on drinking her tea. They always drink tea in the kitchen; all day and all night long they drink this tea. They must be like bladders.

'Where's dear little Amos?' I asked and picked up a cat.

'Playing in his nursery like a well-behaved little boy,' she said tartly.

'He *is* a dear little boy,' I said; 'I just *love* that Amos character.'

I could see she didn't trust me.

'If you like him so well why were you all so nasty to him, then?' she asked.

'We weren't,' I said; 'we were playing mothers and fathers with Miss D. She put on a man's voice and made like she was the father. It was the hell of a good game.'

'What *language*!' she muttered.

'Well, it was the hell of a good game,' I said, 'call it what you like. He clung onto Elizabeth's pants and they fell apart and he fell into these cowpats; it was his own fault.'

'Fell into *what*?' she asked, her eyes blazing.

'Cowpats,' I said, quite simply.

'Really!' She was shocked, she was honestly.

'I expect Amos wondered who that man was up there. Pretty funny when all the time it was poor old Miss D. being a father.'

'Is that who you had up there, then?' she asked. Her mouth hung open and I could see her bottom plate.

'Who else?' I asked.

'Might have been that convict they're looking for,' she said.

'You don't think we'd entertain a murderer un-awares, do you?' I asked, and had a good big laugh. 'You don't think we'd do anything but run like ants if we thought we'd got a murderer in our old oast, do you?' I asked.

She stared at me. I told you she hates my guts.

Before she could say any more Cookie came in.

'Hullo, Cookie,' I said. 'Hullo, good old Cookie; you're just the wonderfullest Cookie in the whole world, that's all,' and I hugged her.

'You'll kill yourself with that Alka-Seltzer,' she said.

I laughed.

'Your father wants you in the sitting-room,' she said, 'you and the others.'

That wiped the laugh off my face. I didn't like the sound of that one.

'What for?' I asked easily enough.

'He wants a word with you,' she said and opened the frig. I hate the smell of frigs, so I went.

Father was sitting at his desk.

A bad sign. Grown-ups always sit at desks when they're going to blow you. They like having pens and things to doodle with so they don't have to face you.

Swallow was by the fire. She shrugged her shoulders, and she picked Bette Davis up and started messing around with her ears. For such a small dog she has huge ears, she has really.

'Yes, Father?' I started.

'Ah—' He made like he didn't know we were there. 'Cookie tells me that Amos Nodge's nurse is here with an odd tale.' He looked across at us.

'Amos says he heard a strange man talking to you kids in one of the barns or somewhere tonight.'

Tonight! That's torn it!

'You mean this afternoon, don't you, Father? When we were playing with Miss D. You saw us yourself. "Unhand her", you said, didn't you?'

I was playing for time.

'I'm talking about tonight; and quite incidentally Miss D. was in East Grinstead all afternoon.'

'She couldn't have been,' I said lamely, very lamely.

'Now look here, you two—' He looked round suddenly. 'Where's the boy?'

'He'll be here in a moment; he went over to the gardener's cottage to take back Elfred's pump.' I lied myself silly.

'Did you or did you not see a strange man?'

We crossed our fingers.

'No,' we said together.

'Afraid I don't believe you.' He got up and crossed over to us. 'It beats me how you can be such fools. Here are the police telling you there's a dangerous convict about, and you won't help by telling the truth.'

He paused and we said nothing.

I felt ghastly. Ghastly. This Alka-Seltzer for once had done me the dirty. I felt as full as hell of bubbles.

'Look here, you kids, can't you trust me?' he asked suddenly.

'We want to,' I said miserably.

'Come on, then. Tell your old Dad all about it. I won't eat you.'

He smiled encouragingly.

'If we told you a secret would you swear to keep it?' I asked. I couldn't stand up much longer with these bubbles in me.

'That depends,' he said.

'Well then,' I said, rather cheekily, I s'pose, 'we can't trust you, can we, since you asked?'

He looked nonplussed. Nonplussed.

'We want to tell you our secret. But we won't if you don't swear to keep it,' I said menacingly.

'Is it about this man?' he asked.

We didn't answer.

'Because maybe it's my business to tell someone else, and then where would I be if I'd sworn? Because if I promise a thing, I keep it. You know that.'

We did.

He looked at us hard for a long time.

We looked stony.

'All right,' he said suddenly, 'I promise.'

We were taken a bit off guard.

We were suspicious.

'Come on, then,' he said, 'I've given you my word.'

'You tell,' I said to Swallow. I didn't dare.

'There *is* a man about,' she said softly. 'Not what you think, though – not a convict.'

'Who then?' asked Father.

'Jesus.'

'*What!*' His eyes nearly dropped out.

'Yes,' I said, 'Jesus.'

He looked astounded.

'I don't understand. You mean a man told you he was Jesus?'

'Well, yes and no,' I said. 'We all know Him to be that, and when you know something is true you just believe it.'

'What made you believe Him to be Jesus?' he demanded.

'Oh, there's proof all right; but beyond that, He's such a jolly nice chap . . . sweet to all of us, quite a heart throb,' I said.

'What's the proof?'

'He has nail-marks in His feet,' said Swallow through Bette Davis' fur.

'Good God!' he sort of whispered to himself.

'You see, we've known Him for quite a long time. Days really, but we didn't tell anyone because . . . well . . . grown-ups don't believe much in Jesus, do they?' I asked him.

He stared. Just stared.

'Why d'you think that?' he asked.

'It's obvious grown-ups don't believe in anything or anyone much . . . Even Granny said if someone called themselves Jesus she'd think they were a lunatic.'

'Hmmm,' he said. 'This sure is a right and left . . .'

What he meant I didn't know.

'You'd like Him. You'd like Him awfully. We do,' said Swallow. 'And nothing and no one but Himself will convince us He's anything or anyone else.'

'I see,' he said, but he clearly didn't.

No one spoke, and then Poor Baby came in. He looked pretty hot and sweaty for a chap who'd just delivered a pump.

'Do you believe in this Jesus talk?' Dad asked.

Poor Baby looked surprised.

'Oh yes, most certainly,' he said. 'Do you?'

'I don't know what to believe,' said Father. 'I've been hit in the solar plexus.'

'Who by?' asked Poor Baby anxiously.

Dad didn't answer him.

'Where is this man?' he asked me.

'Can't tell you now,' I said. 'He might be anywhere.'

'Has Dad joined the Society?' asked Poor Baby.

'In a way,' we said. 'Anyway, he's sworn to secrecy.'

'That's all right, then,' said Poor Baby and wiped his face with the tail of his shirt.

Dad sat with his head in his hands. He looked flattened out. Then he went over to the table and helped himself to the bottle.

He'll be okay now, I thought to myself.

The phone went and he picked it up.

'There's a police car at the bottom of the drive,' Poor Baby whispered. 'They're at Edward's house, Crikky told me.'

'Hullo,' said Dad on the phone.

We listened.

'Oh . . . really?' said Dad on the phone. 'Did he? . . . What else? . . . I see . . . I see . . . I see . . .'

133

God knows what he saw. We didn't like the sound of it.

'Well . . . if you say so . . . though I don't think . . . Hardly, I think . . . no . . . yes . . . really? . . . No, it's just that I'm . . . well . . . I see . . . of course, Inspector . . . anything you say . . . but I really don't want the children . . . hmm . . . hmm . . . hmm . . . No, nothing at all odd . . . well . . . all right . . . bye.'

He hung up and faced us.

We waited.

'Your friend Nodge told his father he heard you talking to a man in the oast . . . asking him if he were a convict or not . . .'

Our friend! I like that . . .

'Well?' He waited.

'We were talking to this man we told you about. Jesus,' said poor Swallow. She was nearly in tears.

'What's happening?' I asked.

'Well . . . naturally the police must explore every avenue. It's their job. If it's not the man they're looking for, we're all right.'

'We?' asked Swallow.

'Yes, all of us. It would be wonderful. Just what the world wants.' He seemed miserable as hell about it.

'When are they coming?' I asked, feeling sick again.

'In a few minutes.' He stood with his back to us at the window. 'If . . . supposing . . . you've made a mistake . . . and people can and do . . . you won't take it badly . . . will you . . . won't stop believing and all that? . . .'

We didn't know what to say.

'I wish you had a mother,' he said quietly. 'I'm not

much good as a mother . . . it's mothers who tell you the right things about God and Jesus . . . you must forgive me if you feel I've failed you in any way, I mean that . . .' He still stood with his back to us.

We didn't answer because quite frankly the conversation had got beyond us; and, anyway, we were a bit worried about our friend in the oast.

'Kids are funny things,' he said suddenly. 'Playing around with toys and things . . . one forgets that they're growing up all the time, with beliefs and ideals . . . and things.'

He was wasting our time, he was really.

'Are the others all ready?' I whispered to Poor Baby.

'More than ready,' he said. 'That police car speeded us up; there are kids tearing all round the place at this moment. Telephones going, and everything.'

Hell, I thought selfishly . . . another bad night.

'Do you miss not having a mother?' Dad asked suddenly. He still had his back to us.

'What?' I asked. 'Good Lord, no. We don't need anyone except ourselves – and you, of course,' I said, trying to be polite.

Father let out a great sigh.

'I think I'll go and find Granny,' he said suddenly.

We knew there wasn't any point asking him not to tell her, and the world would be full of police in a moment. We all had to do our nuts, that's all.

He paused at the door.

'Oddly enough, only today I was wondering if you wouldn't all love to go to boarding school,' he said brightly.

'What the hell would that prove?' I asked rudely.

Any other time he'd have been livid. But this time he just opened the door and went out.

This was our chance.

In a flash we were out of the room and down towards the oast.

Actually we were going in to warn Him.

Something stopped us, and it wasn't a police car either. It was children.

Hundreds of them. Never seen so many. Didn't know half of them even.

Shirley and the usual crowd were in the front and Tracy and Max. It was pretty dark, and no light anywhere.

'What's going on?' we whispered.

'Crikky heard the inspector tell Edward what old Amos had said. He was also there when the inspector phoned your Father. We didn't miss a moment or a trick,' said Jeremy. 'Mark flew off on his bike and used Elizabeth's phone because they're all out. They've come from every-where . . . as far as Tunbridge Wells!' he said excitedly.

On the other side the old oast stood out against the sky with a few corny stars in it. We didn't even know if He was still there.

'Is He still there?' I asked.

'Elizabeth says He is,' said Pippa. 'He doesn't give a hoot.'

'It's part of the plan for Him to be taken again and again,' said Swallow wearily.

'Well, this time He's got us,' I said. God, I felt full of bubbles.

'Get everyone into the hedges and hide behind barns,' Swallow whispered. 'We mustn't let anyone know what's going on.'

We must have waited in the cold behind this old Italian creeper for hours. Even the doves were anxious and fretting up in their dovecote. I was cold as hell and just terrified I'd get hiccoughs.

We heard Father and Cookie and Granny calling, and the lot of them were just advancing with sticks and lanterns when this police car came up and stopped.

'Well, we know where he is,' said old Porkers; 'the boy Nodge told us.'

'I wonder if he got some pieces of silver?' Dad said.

'What's that, sir?' asked Porkers, but Dad only laughed.

Quite right, he was thinking of that character Judas.

There was a lot of muttering that we couldn't hear on account of this Italian creeper being in the way.

There were five of these Porkers-type policemen, but they didn't have guns like they do on television.

They advanced slowly in line towards the oast, and just about as they arrived beside the cow-house there was a shrill whistle from Poor Baby.

They stopped and stared. Personally I think they were scared stiff.

Then Porkers stepped forward and shouted:

'Come on out, Blake . . . we know you're there!'

Blake! How silly can you get!

There was nothing but silence . . . no answer . . . He shouted again. Then he switched on the most gigantic torch I ever saw. Fascinating really.

He stopped.

Right there in the beam of his torchlight were what seemed to be hundreds of children.

They filled up the whole yard between him and the oast, and everyone wore these badges.

He was shocked. Quite shocked. But held. He pulled himself together.

'Come on, kids,' he shouted. 'Out of the way; we mean business.'

Brute.

No one moved. They were solid, and by now we were in the crowd too, with this light shining in our eyes.

If you'd wanted to move you couldn't because you couldn't see where the heck you were going.

'Come on, get weaving,' he shouted patronisingly.

No one moved.

'It's no use standing there gaping. We're after a convict. Clear out,' he said, 'or we'll use force.'

We were hypnotised.

'Go on, Bert,' he yelled, 'push them out of the way . . . What the hell do they think they're doing, anyway?'

This Bert started to try and push, but he pushed the wrong boy. It was Brian; he's a giant of about six foot five . . . I don't s'pose he knew what the hell was going on, but he didn't like being pushed and he knocked the fellow down.

'Easy, easy, now,' yelled Porkers. 'You don't want to follow the man up there, do you?'

'We do,' we shouted.

Lovely; it was getting fun now and liable to be rough.

'For He's a jolly good fellow,' someone shouted, and before you knew where we were, everyone was singing 'For He's a jolly good fellow' and stamping their feet. Must have warmed his heart-strings.

Try as they might they couldn't shift us, and I was glad to see Father wasn't on their side. Nor did he give us any orders.

It was *then* that the most *extraordinary* thing happened.

The barn and the oast broke out in flames!

'Get the fire brigade!' shouted Porkers. 'It's probably a faulty connection somewhere, but it might be Blake up to his old tricks.'

Everyone seemed to be tearing round in circles. Another police car had driven up and a rather grand sort of policeman who looked more like St John's Ambulance strode across the yard as if everything belonged to him.

Porkers was carrying on like mad, and talking and waving his hands about to this St John's Ambulance type man, who just stood about saying things we couldn't hear.

'Another thing,' we heard Porkers say, 'if these kids won't get out of the way the fire brigade can hose them out of the way! Never come across such a ridiculous situation in me life!'

In the distance we could see old Granny; her hair was sticking out all round her head where the wind had caught it. She looked like something out of our fairytale book. She was waving madly at nothing, but if she was yelling we couldn't hear a word she was saying. Father was just standing there with Violet and old Cocky. They seemed in another world, they did really.

By now the oast was pretty well burning hard; great flames were shooting out of one side of it, and we could see figures all over the place, black, like cut-outs we have in a book in the nursery.

Everyone seemed to be about. All the men, looking ghastly and running around to see the fire wasn't reaching this cowshed.

'Thank Gawd there ain't no calves in there,' I heard someone say. I don't know who it was.

Porkers had himself a megaphone now.

'Are you children going to get out of our way!' he bellowed.

'NO!' came a great shout. 'NO . . . NO . . . NO . . .'

'Dammit,' I heard him say, 'where are all their mothers and fathers! Get some fool to find out and clear them away.'

By now it seemed to me there were even more. Total strangers all wearing the badge, so I couldn't complain.

'Where are you from?' I asked a black-headed boy standing by me.

'From Dorking,' he shouted back. 'I got off the bus with the others at the crossroads when I heard the news.'

Dorking! That's the end of the world.

'How did you know?' I shouted at him. 'Who told you?'

'I dunno,' he said; 'one tells another and another tells another and all of a sudden thousands know. That's how it was on the bus.'

The St John's looking man was picking his nose. It was the only sign of emotion he showed, except he kept looking at Porkers and then at Father. But Father didn't move. He just stood staring, unbelievably really.

Swallow had got sort of cut off. I could see her, but I couldn't get at her. Poor Baby was still beside me, and I hung on to his hunk of hair. I suddenly didn't want anything to happen to him with all this fire and everything.

'What you got in your shirt?' I shouted.

'Bette Davis!' he shouted back.

It was like Guy Fawkes night, it was really. Only better.

Crikky was pretty near me too, and I yelled at him:

'D'you think He's all right up there?'

'Sure . . . quite sure . . . it's a miracle,' he said, and it was the first time I really thought he believed.

In a second his word went round: Miracle . . . miracle . . . miracle. . . . I could hear it everywhere, and all their faces were shining in the light of the fire.

Suddenly two huge fire engines arrived.

Phew!

You never saw anything so exciting in your life.

'Never mind the fire, hose those children out of the way!' this Porkers creature was shouting.

'What a performance!' said Poor Baby.

That's when Father moved. In a second he was on this fire engine. He knew old Harold, and old Harold respected him.

'Direct the hose straight at that oast, Harold,' he said, 'straight at it.'

'Blimey!' Harold was saying. 'What an audience! Never seen so many kids in me whole life. Where they come from?'

'All over the world, Harold,' Poor Baby shouted; 'all over the world.'

There was total confusion by now. Men hosing the oast like mad, their gigantic helmets shining in the light of enormous lamps, policemen running round in circles, and always this vast crowd of more and more children.

'It's like the Pied Piper of Hamelin all over again,' I heard old Cocky say, and for the first time he didn't seem to be sending anything up.

'Hope to God he doesn't spirit them all away in the same fashion,' I heard Dad reply. 'Don't know what I'd do without my idiots.'

I could see Swallow was amazed. She kept making faces at me over other people's heads. The whole thing had gone beyond us, it really had. Almost frightening really.

The hose was pouring water onto the oast; one side of it was quite burnt away, but it didn't seem to be coming any nearer to us. I wondered afterwards if anyone would have moved. They were solid down that end, and not a squawk out of anyone, and all the time our corny old doves were flying round and round it, round and round it, like they were on the Dodgems or something.

'Look at old Stanley,' Poor Baby called to me. 'Look at holy old Stanley!'

There were other people arriving now – people with huge cameras like News Reels. Excited as hell they were, pushing and shoving and clambering up on the old Italian creeper and taking pictures of all these children.

'What is it?' I heard one of them say.

'If you don't know, why do you take pictures?' a voice answered.

'Always first with the news, good or bad,' the man said, and then he seemed to fall down; we never saw him again.

Everyone was swaying about. There wasn't all that room. I fought my way to the swing and found about twelve people on it.

Half the rhododendron bush was broken, and there were people just everywhere.

I was suddenly sick of it. I was really.

As suddenly as the fire started, it stopped. I s'pose it was these hoses.

Quick as lightning Porkers and the other policemen were across the yard and into the oast.

There was nothing more we could do about it. Nothing.

We waited. Waited in silence. Hundreds of us, the lights shining on our badges. Nobody moving. If we'd been trained to stand still we couldn't have done better.

'At least we held them up,' Jeremy said.

I saw Father walk slowly across the yard. He looked very old all of a sudden, I don't know why. Maybe it was the light.

He disappeared into the oast.

Still none of us moved.

We just waited. I don't know what for.

After a few moments Father appeared at the door of the oast. He stood quite still for a moment, and then he said not too loudly:

'Will my three children please come here?'

There was no problem to get there. People just fell back and let us pass.

We held each other's hands as we went. We were terrified suddenly that we were going to find Him all dead and burnt.

I remember looking at Poor Baby and thinking his head looked as if it was on fire, but of course it was only all that red hair.

We walked steadily across the yard. Personally I felt as if we were going to be shot.

'Yes, Father?' we whispered nervously.

'Come with me,' he said and started up the ladder.

I looked over my shoulder and saw all these hundreds of children's faces watching.

We climbed up slowly one after the other and found ourselves in the top of the oast.

One side of it was burnt down and we could see the sky quite easily and all these stars.

Old Porkers had his bright torch and was messing about in the straw and poking bits of half-burnt apples. Everything smelled very odd.

There was no one else.

Not a sign of anyone, either burnt or alive. Not a sign that anyone had been there.

Old Porkers rattled down the ladder, shouting out something we couldn't hear.

'What are we doing here, Father?' asked Swallow.

'Wanted you to see this,' he said, and pointed to the bit of the wall that was still standing.

He held up his torch for us to see, and we looked.

On the white wall was a little black cross. Like you see in churches. It looked as if someone had drawn it with his thumb – you know, thick, with dust from the floor.

There wasn't a sign of anything else at all.

'I thought you'd like to see that,' said Father, 'then you can tell the others if you want to.'

Then he went down the ladder.

'That was His goodbye sign,' Swallow said sadly. 'You know, like the Vicar makes at us at the end of church on Sundays, when he says ". . . be among you and remain with you always".'

'Who's going to tell all those others?' asked Poor Baby.

'I don't want to,' I told him. 'I'd be scared stiff and wouldn't know what to say, anyway.'

'Well, they *should* know,' he added. 'Some of them have come absolute *miles*, all the way from *Dorking*!'

'What the heck can you say?' I asked. I was looking round the oast; soon the rain would get in and it would be all nasty.

'Look,' said Swallow, 'there's that flower that Johnnie brought up, all beastly and wet.'

'What can we say to them out there?' Poor Baby persisted.

'Just say it's the end of the story,' I replied.

'S'posing it isn't?' he asked. 'And, anyway, who *is* going to tell them?'

'Go on, Brat,' said Swallow; 'you're a writer, aren't you?'

'Writing and speaking is two different things,' I told her a trifle loftily. I was beginning to sweat at the idea, I was really. All those faces!

'Come on,' Poor Baby said. 'Let's get it over and make it short and sweet; I'm dead beat, I am really.'

We went down the ladder. Father was waiting outside with some of the farm men and old Edward. They looked anxious, I thought, wondering what we were going to say, and who was going to say it.

'Come on, you,' said Edward, 'you're the most talkative,' and before I knew it I was up on his shoulder.

I could see everyone. It was ghastly.

Thousands of eyes glaring at me in this oddish light, like wild animals in the dark, only they didn't go all phosphorus like cats' or lions'.

There wasn't a sound anywhere.

Edward sort of nudged my behind. I was racking my brains for something to say.

'One side of the joint up there is burnt away,' I began. Hell, I thought. 'You can see the sky and the stars . . . He's not there any more, of course . . . Well, we didn't expect Him to be—'

Still there wasn't a sound anywhere.

I *had* to go on:

'The side what is *not* burnt away has a sign on it. You know, like people make on trees to show they went this way, so you know which way to follow – a cross.'

Still not a single soul said a word or made a movement. Golly, I thought, how long is this going on? They're all listening like mad and I don't know what the heck to say next.

'We could stick this sign on our badges if there's any room,' I drooled on.

Weren't the fools ever going to move?

'Well . . . like those French Underground men stuck all over the place . . . you know . . . to show they were free. . . .'

They all started nodding their heads, which was something active at least.

'So . . . well . . . He's free, isn't He? There isn't any more to say, and you can all go home to Dorking and places. . . .'

I'd had enough. I had really. I struggled down, and then suddenly everyone started cheering. Extraordinary, really.

They all moved off after that, and pretty soon there wasn't anyone left except a few old cronies like Jeremy and Co. and Tracy and Max.

'Hey,' said Max, 'what about Amos? If we see him, shall we give him a bit of a caning?'

'Golly, no!' I answered. 'Just be dignified, and turn the other cheek, sort of thing.'

'Okay,' said Max disappointedly, 'but it isn't often you get a bone fide reason for bashing a chap.'

Lucky devil; I noticed he went off in the police car. I bet he gonged the hell out of everyone all the way home.

'Come on,' said Father; 'bed.'

I'm here to tell you I was pretty pleased at the idea. My back was hurting like mad.

Edward carried me all the way upstairs and plonked me on my bed. He's as strong as a giant, he is really.

'Edward,' said Poor Baby, 'd'you s'pose He was just going to play noughts and crosses with Himself?'

'No,' said Edward emphatically, 'I do not, and don't you ever think anything else but what Brat said.'

'What did she say?' he asked. 'I'm so tired I've forgotten really.'

'She said it was like a sign on a tree, to show which way to go if you wanted to follow.'

'What if you're too tired to go any farther?' asked Poor Baby.

'Then you just sits down and waits,' said Edward.

There were hot-water bottles in the bed for a change. Bette Davis was insane about mine. She'd got pretty cold out there with her corny sort of fur.

The grown-ups came in to say goodnight. All of them. No one smelled funny; there hadn't been time for the golden bottle.

'Look here,' said Father, 'I don't want you to be upset about your chum out there.'

'Good Lord, no,' said Swallow. She was putting her nightie on back to front – on purpose, I knew that. It's torn in front and a bit low for someone of her age. *You know* . . .

'How d'you feel about it all?' Father went on.

'Smashing,' said Poor Baby.

'About Him, I mean,' went on Father.

'Oh,' said Swallow, 'he just got away, that's all. Don't let's go *on* about it.'

She wasn't concentrating. She had this tail of her nightie caught round her neck.

'You see, Dad,' I explained as kindly as I could, 'it just wasn't the right time. You could see by all that din and fuss that the police were making that there wasn't a hope of Him getting any grown-ups to believe . . . so He just went. . . .'

'What about all those kids?' asked Violet. 'I'll never forget all those kids' faces as long as I live, out there in that firelight.'

'The kids are all right,' I told her. My back was beginning to be murder. 'They all believed. One day, when *we're* all grown-ups, He's coming back again. Then we'll be ready.'

'Peter Pan all over again,' said old Cocky under his breath.

I didn't know what he was talking about, so I asked for some Horlicks. That's what I wanted more than anything, even Alka-Seltzer. I could have died for Horlicks.

'Good old Brat!' said Poor Baby. 'I knew there was something I was longing for, and I didn't know what it was. It's Horlicks, that's what it is.'

'I'll send it up,' said Father, as he kissed us goodnight, and they all went out.

We could hear them talking as they went down the stairs.

'Amazing!' said Granny. 'They've dismissed it already in their minds.'

'What do you make of it, Slim?' asked Violet.

'There are more things in heaven and earth, dear Violet, than are dreamt of in your philosophy.'

Grown-ups do make the most extraordinary remarks.

'Here,' I called to the others, who were in the bathroom, 'what you two up to?'

'Teeth,' said Poor Baby through the brush.

'Pretty silly when you haven't even had the Horlicks,' I shouted back. 'I don't want any old holes in my teeth, if you do.'

They came out.

'What is it?' asked Swallow.

'I'm going to make that same mark that He did, and not on my badge neither. Right here, over my perishing bed.'

'Goodo,' said Poor Baby. 'So will I.'

And we all did.

I got out my diary after that to put a circle round the day so I wouldn't forget. Then I noticed something.

'Hey,' I said, 'what does it say about today in your two diaries?'

They got them out.

'Mine says Fox Hunting begins,' said Swallow.

'Mine says "Order your wafer now",' said Poor Baby. 'Why? What does yours say?'

'All Hallows Eve,' I told him. 'That's what it says, All Hallows Eve.'

'So what?' asked Poor Baby.

'It doesn't make any sense,' Swallow said. 'Because you're s'posed to bob for apples, and we haven't. You're s'posed to look in a mirror at midnight and see who you're going to marry, and we haven't.'

'There's still time,' said Poor Baby. 'I'd like to, in fact . . . I'm not so sure of Elizabeth after all.'

'Odd things happen on All Hallows Eve,' I told them.

'You can say that again,' said Poor Baby. 'Because odd things *have*.'

Father brought up the Horlicks and sat on the bed while we drank it.

'What *exactly* does All Hallows Eve mean, Father?' I asked him.

'It means Hallowmas,' he said very quietly. 'It's the evening before All Saints' Day.'

'Sort of queer, isn't it?' I said, giving the remains of my cup to Bette Davis. 'And, incidentally, as we're alone now . . . did *you* believe?'

'I believe that I did,' he said.

Then he went.

We lay still in our beds, and there wasn't any more after that.

It was warm in my bed, and I thought of Jesus, and where He was. . . . The barn and the oast would be emptier now than they were before He came. . . .

Outside in the sky, and in the room, there was no colour, just grey, like shadders, and over the farmhouse this night swam like a great moonlit sea. . . .

The dark was all around us. There wasn't a sound anywhere. Not even the washing-up noises.

Darkness . . . all around us. . . . But we weren't alone. That's all. . . .

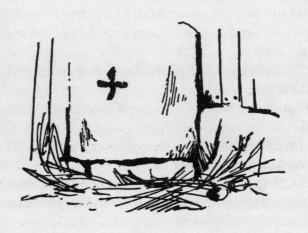

From the Author

One lovely morning in the summer of 1957 I was sitting in my gypsy caravan at our farm in Sussex, waiting for inspiration. It came suddenly, out of the blue, *Whistle Down the Wind*. The beginning, the middle, the end – the complete story.

In a few days it was finished, my publisher had bought it and it was on its way to the bookshelves. My children, Juliet, Hayley and Jonathan, loved it and, of course, being quite intelligent, recognised themselves. Later on my grand-children also enjoyed it and now, because of this lovely new edition, my great granddaughter, Cheyanne, will, I hope, enjoy it too.

This recent letter said: 'Dear Lady Mills, I enjoy reading books and listening to stories very much indeed. My Dad recently gave me a cassette of *Whistle Down the Wind*. I thought it was wonderful. It was so exciting. I'm really pleased that we never knew whether Jesus was the escaped convict. I don't believe he was. I talked to my Dad and he thought he was. Me, I'm with Brat. Thank you so much for your terrific story. I shall always remember it. With lots of love from Tom Attenborough (aged 9. The elder son of your husband's godson!).'

The book really does seem to have been born under a lucky star. In 1961 our great friends Dickie Attenborough (now His Lordship) and Bryan Forbes made a delightful film of it. The picture turned out to be a great success and now, to my amazement, Andrew Lloyd Webber has bought it to produce a musical stage version before making it as a film.

To say I am a lucky author is the understatement of the year!

Mary Hayley Bell
October 1996

PS. My husband has read this and wants me to say it is one of his favourite books but, of course, since we have already celebrated our Golden Wedding anniversary, he has to be, shall we say, slightly biased!